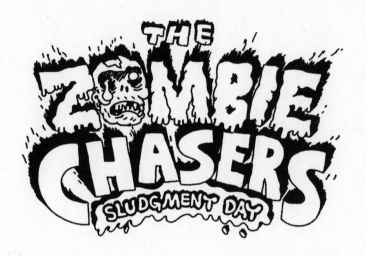

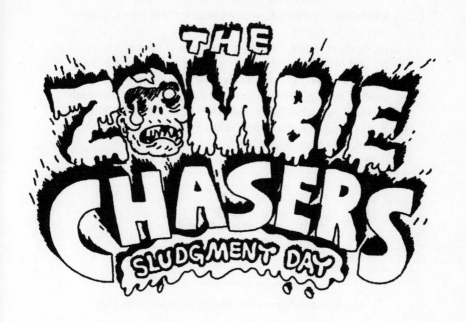

THE ZOMBIE CHASERS
SLUDGMENT DAY

BY JOHN KLOEPFER
ILLUSTRATED BY
STEVE WOLFHARD

HARPER
An Imprint of HarperCollinsPublishers

The Zombie Chasers: Sludgment Day
Copyright © 2011 by Alloy Entertainment and John Kloepfer

www.harpercollinschildrens.com

Produced by Alloy Entertainment
151 West 26th Street, New York, NY 10001

Library of Congress Cataloging-in-Publication Data

Kloepfer, John.
  Sludgment day / by John Kloepfer ; illustrated by Steve
Wolfhard. — 1st ed.
    p. cm. — (The zombie chasers ; 3)
  ISBN 978-0-06-185310-4
[1. Zombies—Fiction. 2. Survival—Fiction. 3. Humorous
stories.] I. Wolfhard, Steve, ill. II. Title.
PZ7.K8646SI 2012   2011022930
[Fic]—dc23   CIP
                                                        AC

12 13 14 15 16 CG/RRDH 10 9 8 7 6 5 4 3 2 1

First Edition

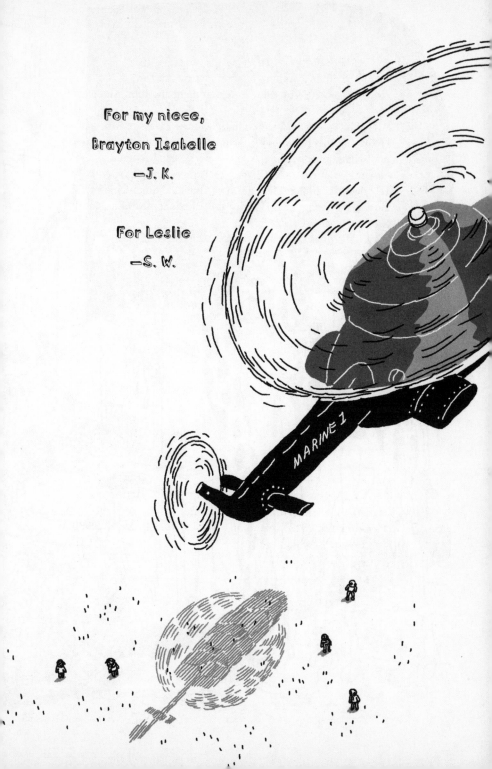

For my niece,
Brayton Isabelle
—J. K.

For Leslie
—S. W.

CHAPTER

The black Secret Service helicopter jetted under the clouds as a sea of walking dead ravaged the landscape below.

Inside the chopper, Zack Clarke stared out the curved windshield, watching the full moon vanish from the sky, then reappear like a magician's coin trick. It was late. Or was it early? Zack had been losing track of time since the zombie outbreak on Friday night. It was Sunday, and he was exhausted, hopelessly praying for the moment when he would wake up from this undead nightmare, back in his own room in Arizona. But that wasn't going to happen. That was one thing he knew for sure.

Zack was riding shotgun next to Ozzie Briggs in the cockpit of the helicopter they had commandeered after escaping the zombified White House with the antidote. Zack's sister, Zoe; her BFF, Madison Miller; his best buddy, Rice; and Dr. Scott, the ginkgo-sedated zombie scientist, were all resting in the back of the chopper. Madison's puppy, Twinkles, snored contently in his owner's lap.

"Where are we now?" Zoe asked, her voice a little weary.

Ozzie pointed to a red radar blip blinking over a neon green map of North America. "Near Memphis, Tennessee." An orange light ticked on the control board, and Ozzie's eyes flicked down to the fuel gauge. He shifted the levers and hit a few buttons. The chopper began to descend.

"Gotta gas up," Ozzie explained, as they cruised just above the treetops.

Beneath the branches, a swarm of flesh-eating lunatics prowled through the streets, bellowing in the gloomy moonlight. Zack twisted around in his seat and peered in the back. Rice was asleep with his head tipped back and his mouth hanging open. "Pssst, Rice . . . wake up! We're about to land."

Rice shot up with a start, squinty-eyed with sleep, and wiped a driblet of drool from his chicken-pocked chin. "PFC Johnston Rice, reporting for duty, sir!" He brought his right hand to his forehead and chopped downward with a sleepy salute that whacked Zoe squarely on her thigh.

"Ow, you little punk!" Zoe flicked Rice hard in the ear. "Watch it!"

"Dang, Zo!" Rice clutched the side of his head.

"Shhhh!" Madison snarled angrily from her wheelchair, still weak from a barrage of blood tests and serum samples in the secret White House laboratory—not to mention the nasty bite wound Greg Bansal-Jones had left on her leg back in Tucson. "Some of us are trying to recuperate," Madison grumbled and dozed back to sleep.

Zack gazed out the cockpit window as they flew over a used car lot and some fast food joints, angling toward a glowing Shell gas station sign with its first letter blacked out.

Ozzie lowered the chopper over the roof covering the fuel pumps, and they touched down.

"Why are we landing up here?" Zack asked.

"Better to stay above ground level," Ozzie said. "Come on, we gotta do this quick." Ozzie grabbed his crutches off the floor and then leaped from the cockpit, balancing on his good leg.

Zack hopped onto the flat gravelly roof and stared across the open view. The sky was pitch-black, but the darkness was alive with the moans and howls of the living dead.

Rice and Zoe jumped down from the chopper, too, and threw the rope ladder off the side of the roof. Ozzie climbed down first.

"Ladies first," Zoe said, gesturing at Rice to go ahead.

Rice made a face with his

tongue stuck out and climbed down after Ozzie.

Zack followed his sister, edging backward nervously until he found one of the rungs with his foot. *Here we go again* . . . , he thought, wobbling fifteen feet in the air.

Zack let out a grunt as his feet hit the ground. He scanned the darkened perimeter. No zombies in sight, but the stink of death and decay quickly filtered through his nostrils. He choked on the scent as the shadows slowly came into focus.

The leprous goons staggered into the dim neon glow surrounding the gas station. "I see dead people," Rice joked.

"Listen up," Ozzie barked, slamming something into Zack's chest. "Buy us a little time with these flares while . . . hold up, Zoe, gimme your mom's credit cards.

Then bring those over here!" He aimed his crutch at a display of red gas cans stacked on the sidewalk in front of the store.

"Excuse me, Mr. Bossypants." Zoe flung the handbag at him and strutted away to fetch the empty gas jugs. A zillion zombies closed in around them, their shredded arms spread wide open, their lips shriveled back, barking mucus and sputtering phlegm. It was gross.

"Ready?" Zack gave Rice a fist bump.

"Time for a little crowd control," Rice said, lighting the flares. He handed one to Zack and they took off in opposite directions.

Straight ahead, an elderly zombie man lumbered toward Zack.

"This way, gramps!" Zack called out to the undead geezer. The zombie sneered back at him, revealing its hideously decomposed chompers. A nasty boil exploded like a lava bubble on the old codger's pulsating cheekbone. Zack wagged the flare in its face and jogged back and forth, shepherding the growing throng of zombies away from Ozzie and Zoe at the gas pumps.

At the other end of the lot, more zombies poured off the roadside, plodding toward the bright pink light. "Hurry up, you guys!" Rice yelled. "I'm dyin' out here!"

"We're going as fast as we can!" Zoe called back.

"Almost done!" Ozzie shouted.

The brain-craving mutants were closing in steadily, forming a dense semi-circle around them. Zack could feel a hundred undead eyes upon him. "How much longer?" he yelled.

"Ahhhhhh!" Rice screamed.

Zack whipped his head around to see his buddy lose control of the zombie flock.

"Rice!" Zack cried, as an undead biker in a black leather vest grabbed Rice's leg and yanked him down to the asphalt. Zack gasped at the sight of his best friend being swallowed up by the ravenous mob.

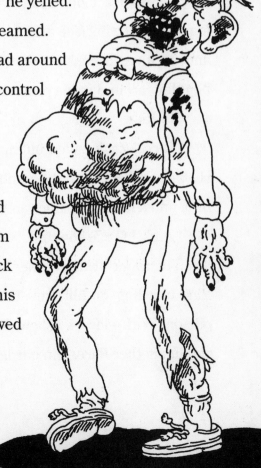

"Zack, look out!" Zoe screamed. "Behind you!"

Zack spun around on his heel. A humongous zombie lunged at him with a double swipe of its colossal arms. Zack ducked then kicked his leg out, tripping the zombified brute, and sent him tumbling to the blacktop with a squishy *splat*.

He whirled around searching for Rice, but all he saw was an endless stream of zombies—a big-bellied butcher with a blood-splattered apron; then a bandy-legged housewife, face dripping with bad plastic surgery; and an undead construction worker with his eyeballs boggling around in his protective goggles.

No Rice.

"Rice!" Zack called out again, sick to his stomach. He backed away from the zombie horde slogging toward him, and a helpless panic ran through his gut. "Rice!"

"Zack!" Ozzie shouted. "Get back in position!"

Then, out of the corner of his eye, there he was: Rice crawling on all fours out of the massive undead pile-on. With glasses askew, Rice scrabbled to his feet and lit another flare. "En garde!" he shouted and struck a fencing stance, galloping in place like a medieval swordsman.

Zack breathed a sigh of relief and went back to work, when suddenly a terrified screech rang out from above. *Madison!* Overhead, Twinkles was barking like crazy, and Zack could see the zombified Dr. Scott thrashing about inside the helicopter. He spun away from the zombie frontline and raced for the rope ladder.

"Ahhhhhh!" Madison shrieked again, and without a second thought, Zack scrambled up the ladder, hoping he wasn't too late.

CHAPTER 2

t the top of the ladder, Zack beelined for the helicopter and then leaped inside the cabin. Madison was cornered in her wheelchair, the ferocious zombie doctor looming over her, about to pounce. Twinkles growled and tugged at the zombie's pant leg, whipping his tiny head back and forth violently.

"*Rargh!*" Dr. Scott slammed her zombie mitts down on Madison's shoulders like a pro wrestler at the start of a match.

"Ew!" Madison shouted and put up her bandaged leg to block the shrieking wretch with the sole of her shoe. "Get offa me, lady!" She grunted and leg-pressed the zombie back to a vertical posture.

Dr. Scott snarled and lashed out, clawing the air in front of Madison's face.

"Hey!" Zack shouted. "Pick on someone your own size!" He took a running leap and latched onto Dr. Scott's back, hanging with his arms wrapped around her neck. He drew his feet up as the zombie snorted and reared like a bucking bronco.

"Hi-*ya*!" Madison kicked the undead doctor stiffly in the stomach. Dr. Scott doubled over, nearly flipping Zack to the floor, but he held on tight as she stumbled backward, crashing into the cockpit.

DOINK! Zack thunked his elbow on a sharp metal corner and cringed with funny-bone pain. *WHAM!* The zombified doctor pinned him against the control board with her back. Zack strained to wriggle free, but the grown-up zombie was too heavy to budge.

"*Blekchle-glugrargh!*" The undead M.D. pawed the controls, groping every switch, button, and dial on the console. Suddenly the helicopter's motor roared to life and the rotors started to spin, ready for takeoff.

"Zack, come on!" Madison yelled over the roar of the engine.

"I'll take care of this, Madison!" Zack shouted. "Just get out of here! Quick!"

Zack lost his grip, and the zombie doctor flipped around and flailed, pulling down the throttle on the steering column.

Madison jumped out of the wheelchair, grabbed Twinkles, and dropped to the rooftop just as the chopper rose into the air. "Zack!" she called, watching the helicopter drift out of control.

Inside the aircraft, Zack socked the undead doctor square in the kisser and squirmed free. He dove back in the cabin. The flight deck seesawed and sent him stumbling headfirst toward the open side hatch. Zack braced himself in the doorframe, peering down at the deadly drop below. He caught a flash of Madison on the roof, clutching Twinkles.

"Zack!" Her scream sounded like a whisper as the chopper arced over the dark horizon.

"Blargh!" The mad zombie doctor staggered wildly

into the cabin. Zack looked down again. The helicopter spiraled over an industrial-size Dumpster filled with black garbage bags.

One . . . two . . . Dr. Scott lunged.

"Three!" Zack plugged his nose and plummeted down through the rank zombie night.

PHLUMP!

Zack landed safely, spread-eagled in the massive trash pile. He lay there for a brief moment, happy to be alive—even in the heap of reeking garbage. That was until something wet seeped through his jeans.

"Ah man," Zack said aloud and lifted his backside. He felt the slimy denim with his hand then sniffed his fingertips and gagged. *Nasty!*

He grabbed a wad of crumpled BurgerDog napkins and daubed at the damp spot when something rustled and squirmed underneath him.

"*Rayrgh!*" A zombie raccoon shot up between Zack's legs, snarling and hissing. Zack scrabbled back as the undead scavenger lunged out of the rubbish and snapped its rabid jaws repeatedly. He grabbed the rim of the Dumpster, hoisted himself up, and dropped down to the cement.

BOOM! A blaze of light flashed and a thick stream of smoke curled up into the clouds. Zack turned his head to see the helicopter burst into flames as it smashed into the median of a divided highway. Dr. Scott clung to the branches of a nearby tree.

Rice and Zoe ran to a stop in front of Zack while Ozzie leaped over on his crutches. The horde of zombies amassed behind them, coming up the rear.

"You're okay, dude!" Rice threw his arms around

Zack and gave him a long, awkward hug. "Man, you scared the crud out of me."

Ozzie grasped Zack on the shoulder. "Thought you were a goner, bro."

"Had to go and be the hero." Zoe glared at her brother coldly. "Now how are we gonna get out of here?" She gestured to the smoldering chopper.

"I coulda almost just died, Zoe!" Zack looked at his sister in disbelief. "So why don't you just shut up?"

"I don't shut up, I grow up; when I look at you, I

throw up." Zoe made a yacking sound and pushed her brother out of her way. Zack quickly shoved his sister right back.

Zoe froze, chuckling to herself. "I know *that* didn't just happen . . . ," she said, then spun around and shoved him twice as hard.

"Do it again," Zack yelled in her face. "I dare you!"

Zoe laughed hysterically.

The tightly packed mob shuffled their way down the cement yard, gurgling and grunting, panting with insatiable hunger.

"Come on, you guys!" Rice shouted, pointing to the zombies.

Zack broke off from Zoe's death stare and they all ran down the side alley. As they ducked around the back corner, Madison called down from the roof of the gas station. "Wait up, people!"

"Madison!" yelled Zack, looking up at the top of the black iron ladder running up the side of the building.

Madison peered down over the ledge. "Here, catch Twinkles." She dropped her puppy and started to climb down herself.

"Arf arf!" Twinkles flailed in the air, landing in Zack's arms.

The little pooch licked his cheek. "Uh-oh . . ." Zack glanced over his shoulder as the massive zombie swarm rounded the corner into the lot behind them.

"Hurry it up, Madison!" Rice shouted.

"She's going as fast as she can, you little runt!" Zoe sniped.

At the head of the pack, a hefty zombie woman unhinged her jaw, ready to gobble up anything in its vicinity. The ghoulish fat woman limped toward them, her arms wide open, wearing pajama pants and a T-shirt with FREE HUGS written on the front.

"Come on!" Rice pleaded. "I'm really not in the mood for hugs right now!"

Madison jumped down off the ladder and stood still, catching her balance, when suddenly her whole body fell slack.

"Whoa!" Zack and Zoe jinxed each other as

Madison fainted. They caught her mid-fall and propped her up on their shoulders.

"*SNAP-Glarghlgle-rrrgh-RAH!*" The zombies stomped closer.

"This way, guys!" Ozzie said, pointing to a service area across a four-lane highway.

"I'm just guessin' here, guys," Rice said, huffing and puffing as they ran past the twisted mass of smoking metal that used to be their helicopter. "But I don't think we're gonna get another chopper that easy, I mean—"

"Rice . . ." Zoe panted, lugging her BFF with her little bro. "Save your breath."

CHAPTER 3

They hustled through the parking lot of a rest stop and pushed through the front doors. Zack and Zoe hauled Madison into the dining area, where a trio of fast food joints lined the far wall—Jim's Steakout, Mighty Taco, and BurgerDog. Madison's feet dragged through the squalor of the demolished food court—spilled fountain sodas mixed with puddles of zombie sludge, squashed hamburgers and half-eaten chicken-finger subs stamped with footprints on the floor, and bits of busted glass and crumpled-up food wrappers littered the entire building.

"Hello?" Rice called out. "Anybody home?"

Nobody answered.

Over by the cash registers, Zack and Zoe lifted Madison onto the BurgerDog counter and laid her flat on her back. Her face was dead asleep. Ozzie held Madison's limp lifeless wrist, checking her pulse.

"Is she gonna be okay?" Zoe asked meekly, worried for her friend.

"She's still breathing," said Zack.

"Check this out!" Rice jogged over from the gift shop, holding two bottles of Madison's all-time favorite drink: kiwi-strawberry VitalVeganPowerPunch. "I can't believe they have this!" Rice stood over Madison and cracked the top off a bottle. He poured a few drops of the pink fruity punch into her mouth and waited.

A few seconds later, her eyelids began to flutter and then popped wide open. Madison smacked her lips and furrowed her eyebrows. "Give that to me. Give it here!" She grabbed the ginkgo drink away from Rice then chugged back the whole bottle in a single gulp. "Kah! . . . Yummy."

They all let out a collective sigh of relief.

"You'll be all right, sweetie," Zoe patted her bestie on the head. "Right now you just need to replenish. What did Dr. Scott call it?"

"Bio-molecular regeneration," Rice said. "She still can't be zombified, but she can't unzombify anybody either right now. We don't know for how long."

"But if she keeps drinking ginkgo," said Zack. "It might speed up the process?"

"I don't know about that," Rice said. "But first things first: I'm starvin' like Marvin!" He put his hands on his hips and studied the chip rack by the sandwich shop with a puzzled frown. "What kind of rinky-dink place doesn't have honey barbecue flavor twists?"

"Ay, Marvin," Zoe said in a bad British accent. "Be a good chap and toss me one of 'em Smartfoods, won't ya, love?"

"One Smartfood, comin' up." Rice tossed her the 99-cent snack pouch, and Zoe pulled it open. She placed a piece of the cheesy popcorn on her tongue and chewed it slowly, staring at her brother. "Want some?" She offered Zack the bag, and he went for it.

"Psych," said Zoe, pulling it out of his reach. "This food is only for smart people." She pointed at the package. "Not for you."

Zack scowled at his sister. "Yeah, then how come *you're* eating it?"

"Guys, chill out, have a Twinkie, okay?" Rice tossed Zack a pack of Twinkies.

Zack unwrapped the yellow snack cake and stuffed it in his mouth, when suddenly—*Briing!* The phone started to ring. Zoe hopped over the counter and picked up the call. "Hello," she said, clamping the phone between her ear and shoulder. "You called me, buddy . . . Who's this? . . . How do you know my brother? . . . Yeah, right, and I'm the tooth fairy." Zoe hung up.

"Who the heck was that?" Zack asked, crinkling his eyebrows.

"Some creep pretending to be the president," Zoe mumbled, biting her nail.

"Zoe, that might have actually been the president," said Zack.

"He did know your name," Zoe scrunched her face.

"Zoe," Ozzie pinched his brow in disbelief. "You just hung up on the commander in chief!"

"Big deal," she said. "He'll call us back." The phone blared again. "See?"

Zack picked up the receiver and put it on speaker. "Um, hello? This is Zack Clarke." The line crackled with static.

"Zachary, this is your president speaking," said the voice on the other end.

"Really?" Zack's voice cracked and he swallowed hard.

"Not so fast, 'Mr. President,'" Rice interrupted, making air quotes around his head with his fingers. "How did you know where we were?"

"We implanted a tracking device in Miss Miller's hospital bracelet . . ."

Madison gasped at the red light bleeping on the plastic band around her wrist.

Rice nodded. "He's the prez."

"What can we do for you, Mr. President?" Ozzie spoke up now.

"My sources tell me you're currently in possession of the antidote," the President said.

Zack patted his shirt pocket, which held the blood-red serum vial.

"And one of our Marine One helicopters."

"Ummm . . ." Zack raised his eyebrows.

"We need you to turn around and head back to Washington."

"With all due respect, Mr. President, sir," Zack said. "We're on our way back to Phoenix to unzombify my parents."

"That wasn't a suggestion," said the President. "That was an order!"

"I'm afraid that's not really gonna be possible, sir," Ozzie said.

"Why not?" asked the President.

"Well," Zack said. "The chopper's kind of sort of . . . out of commission."

"What happened?"

"Zack crashed it, Mr. President," Zoe blurted.

Zack stared at his sister in disbelief.

"What?" she shrugged and whispered innocently. "You did."

There was a long silence before the President spoke again. "Then you're the last chance we've got . . ."

"What does that mean?" Zack asked.

"It means you've just become our primary initiative to reverse the outbreak."

"Um, how do you, like, expect us to do that?" Madison asked.

"Listen closely. You're going to need to make more of the serum. There's a secret lab facility with the capabilities—" The President's voice cut out, replaced by the long bleep of the dial tone.

"Mr. President?" Ozzie shook the phone. "Chief!"

"You guys, this is serious." Zack looked at his friends.

"Seriously," said Madison, twisting a lock of her hair around her finger.

"We need a plan." Zack stroked his chin.

"And what plan is that?" Zoe snapped. "We're in the

middle of nowhere with no ride. We have no idea where the super-secret lab is. All we have is the stupid antidote. And we don't even know what to do with it!"

"Quiet down, Zoe." Ozzie raised his eyebrows. *"They'll* hear you."

"Who?" Zoe asked, looking around dubiously. "It's just us."

"Him." Ozzie lifted his eyes to the vaulted ceiling lined with windows, where a zombie was crawling on the rooftop glass.

"Yeah, guys," Zack whispered. "We can't stay here too long."

"Let's just wait a couple minutes," Rice suggested. "Hopefully the prez'll call back and tell us where to go."

Zack sniffed his armpit and glanced down at the garbage stains on the front of his shirt. "Ugh," he groaned. "I'll be right back."

"Zack, how many times must I remind you? You're not supposed to say that."

"Say what?" Zack said as he strolled away from the food court.

"That you'll be right back," Rice grumbled. "It's like a basic rule of thumb when you're up against a world full of zombies."

"Thanks for the tip, Rice," said Zack. "I'll be back *soon*." He grabbed a clean T-shirt from the gift shop and walked down the corridor. As he entered the men's room he could hear the distant din of the zombie plague droning outside the rest stop.

CHAPTER 4

Zack tiptoed cautiously through the bathroom holding his fresh new T-shirt. When he reached for the faucet, a nasty brown cockroach shot up from the drain and skittered out of the sink. On pure reflex, Zack grabbed an old folded-up newspaper off the countertop and slammed the juicy bug. *SPLAT!* He was checking the splotch of squashed insect guts when the word "BurgerDog" caught his eye in a front-page headline. Zack carefully peeled open the newspaper and started to read:

BURGERDOG CEO UNDER FIRE

Days after an FDA advisory committee approved the use of genetically engineered animals for human food consumption, famed geneticist Thaddeus Duplessis has announced the grand opening of his new fast food chain: BurgerDog. The fledgling franchise features a hamburger that tastes like a hotdog—a BurgerDog—and a frankfurter that tastes like ground beef, called the WeenieBurger.

Four years ago Duplessis earned fame and fortune when he developed the popular canine sub-breed Perma-Pup, a dog that stays a puppy forever. Since then, the geneticist has devoted his talents to this new food chain enterprise.

Located in Billings, Montana, BurgerDog Enterprises produces and manufactures all of its own meat in a state-of-the-art processing facility next door to the ranch where the animals are raised. However, these animals are not your typical livestock. Mr. Duplessis has created a new species, recombining pig DNA with cow DNA and cloning the new genetic hybrid. The result—a bovine hog, as Duplessis has coined it—is where the BurgerDog gets its distinctive pork-beef flavor.

However, animal rights activists are appalled at the lack of testing and evidence that proves genetically engineered animals are safe to eat. And local vegan groups are already organizing protests

outside various BurgerDog locations across the country. Other researchers agree that recombining DNA from two different species can result in unforeseen mutations that may have dangerous side effects.

Duplessis could not be reached for comment.

Zack leaned over the sink and breathed deeply. Duplessis and BurgerDog. BurgerDog and Duplessis. Genetically engineered cow-pigs? Who was this guy? And what about his state-of-the-art processing facility?

That's it!

Zack pulled his stinky shirt over his head and put on the clean one that read I ♥ MEMPHIS. Then he turned on the faucet and cupped his hands full of water. He splashed his face and scrubbed the garbage juice caked on his arms. *Montana, here we come . . .* , Zack thought as he heard a stall door creak open. He turned off the water and glanced up at his reflection in the mirror.

A psychotic zombie beast was gazing over its shoulder, slurping up a rope of slime that dangled off its underbite. Zack froze. His heart skipped a beat. A custardlike blob of green-speckled ooze hung from its nostril, and an aura of stench wavered around its ZZ Top beard. *"Raaaoow!"* The reanimated grimeball let forth a deep guttural howl like Chewbacca the Wookiee.

Zack dropped down to a crouch as the zombie swung its mammoth fist, barely missing Zack's head and smashing the mirror to pieces.

The undead madman stomped straight for him, snapping and gargling.

Zack crabwalked backward into an open stall and hopped back up to his feet. He slammed the stall door shut, locking himself inside, and spun around. He glanced down and gagged at the stench of the unflushed toilet bowl.

WHAM! The filthy beast banged the flimsy door with a loud crash.

Zack leaped up onto the toilet seat and then grabbed the ceiling pipe above him with both hands.

BOOM! The hinges popped off the doorframe. The

burly beast busted into the stall and reached for Zack's swinging legs. Zack flung his feet up on the zombie's shoulders and brought the revolting slob crashing down on the backswing.

The zombie fell face forward into the toilet, and Zack dropped down full force onto its head and shoulders. *KERSPLASH!* The undead goon gurgled into the porcelain bowl, blowing bubbles in the rancid sludge. It was the most unfortunate swirly since middle-school

bully Greg Bansal-Jones dunked Rice at the beginning of the school year.

Zack bounded off the zombie's backside and sprinted for the exit. At the door, he skidded to a stop and doubled back, grabbing the newspaper off the sink counter. He couldn't wait to show his friends what he'd found.

CHAPTER

Zack jogged down the corridor, where he snatched a road map from the info desk and headed back over to the seating area. The undead moan had grown louder, and the zombie on the rooftop pounded its fist on the windowpanes overhead.

"I told you not to go off by yourself," Rice scolded. "Where you been?"

"I had a little scuffle, no biggie," Zack said. "What's going on?"

"No word from the prez," Madison lamented.

Outside, the rest stop was swarming with zombies on all sides.

"We need to get out of here," Zoe said. "Like, now."

"We need a vehicle . . ." Ozzie gazed out the window, pointing beyond the parking lot full of zombies. In the distance a brightly lit car dealership glittered with red, white, and blue flags rippling in the breeze around the top of the fenced-in lot.

Just then, a crash pierced the silence. Shattered glass cascaded down from the ceiling as the rooftop zombie fell to the floor with a crunchy plop. Every one of its joints was dislocated, angling out like a bent-out-of-shape action figure. Its mouth was a black hole with teeth. The kill-crazy cannibal croaked and spattered red specks of disease as it rose up on its pigeon-toed feet. On the other side of the food court, a pack of zombies wedged through the unlocked doors.

"Let's get out of here!" Zack and Rice yelled as they picked up the gas jugs that Zoe filled earlier and lugged them over to the main entrance. The automatic doors slid open, and they all stared out at the zombified boulevard.

Briing! Briiing! Behind them, the phone started ringing again at the cash register. "The prez!" Rice gasped. But it was too late. There was no turning back.

The zombies tottered toward them, hobbling on invisible canes, jerking and convulsing. They moaned and gurgled, *snappity-snap*, gnashing their own tongues into hunks of half-chewed food.

"Ready . . . ," Zoe said.

"Set . . ." Ozzie ground his crutch into the pavement.

"Zombies!" Rice and Zack shouted.

"Arf arf arf!" Twinkles led the charge as they dashed head-on into the zombie mayhem. First there were a dozen, then half a block later an even hundred brain-craving corpses rambled up the road, congesting the sidewalks.

Zack plotted a course and tore up the undead gauntlet, staying low to the ground, running against the one-way zombie foot traffic. A gangly zombie brute wearing a red bandana and a long ponytail zigzagged at Zack with both hands thrust forward. The side of its face looked like a plateful of onion rings. Zack cut to the right, past the flaky-faced miscreant.

To the left, Rice gripped the handle of the gas jug with both hands, spinning around like an Olympic hammer thrower. *BAM!* He clocked a zombie lady in the shins and swept her legs right out from under her.

In front of Rice, Madison scooped Twinkles up and cradled the puppy under her arm like a football. She ran behind Zoe, who carved out a path, kickboxing through the undead psychos in their way.

To the right, a middle-aged zombie fellow rushed at Ozzie. Its swollen head bulged to twice its natural size. Ozzie planted both crutches and swung his injured

leg up—*BLAOW!* He blasted the bulbous-headed freak
in the face with his cast.

Zack sprinted, dodging through the nonstop
barrage of demented zombie mutants, when he heard
Madison let out a high-pitched yelp. He turned his head
and saw an undead high-school girl thrashing wildly at
Madison. Its bent-back finger was tangled in Madison's
hospital bracelet.

"Ick!" Madison shrieked. "It's touching me!" She
ripped her arm back and broke free, but the White House
tracking device snapped off. The bracelet seemed to

hover in midair before it kerplunked down a sewer grate and was gone.

"Ahhh!" A split second later, Zack was kissing the pavement, palms on the ground, scraped up badly. He looked behind him to see where he tripped.

"*Ghlarf! Ghlarf!*" Two zombie pit bulls growled, dragging their undead dog walker by twisted leashes lashed around its decomposing forearms. At the end of its leash, one of the undead dogs bit the air less than a foot from Zack's nose.

Zack scrambled to his feet and spun around to see a crowd of slime-gurgling misfits with their arms outstretched, stomping straight for him.

Zack wheeled around and spotted an abandoned Cadillac with both front doors standing wide open in the middle of the road. He took off and dove headfirst in the passenger side door, just in time to avoid a zombified college kid stumbling by. Zack scooted to the driver's side as the undead frat boy tore the door off its hinges and chucked it into the air. The keys jangled, still in the ignition. *Bingo!* Zack cranked the car key, and the engine began to purr.

"Rargh!" The zombified preppy stuck its face in the passenger side and grappled across the seat. Zack lifted his feet up, with his knees to his chest, and launched a two-footed push-kick into the zombie's slobbering face. *POW!* The undead undergrad toppled back and slammed to the ground.

Zack pulled his own door closed as a five-man zombie platoon staggered toward the Cadillac. To see out the windshield, he stood up and gripped the steering wheel like a ship's captain, then shifted into gear and pressed the accelerator. The car lurched forward, and Zack steered over to his friends, who were fighting an endless battle against the monstrous zombie swarm.

This isn't so hard, Zack thought. *It's like a giant go-cart.* "Get in!" he shouted, poking his head up through the sunroof.

BLAMMO! Zoe rocked a zombie square in the chest

with a straight kick and jogged to the Cadillac along with Ozzie on his crutches.

Rice retreated, too, gazing up at his pal with a look of admiration. "Yo, dude, you're freakin' driving right now!"

"Shotgun!" Madison called and hopped in the door-less passenger seat, carrying Twinkles. Rice jumped in the back with Zoe and Ozzie, who were out of breath after the intense hand-to-hand combat. Zack peeled out quickly, swerving toward a pack of ravenous ghouls tottering in front of them.

"Don't hit them!" Madison reached across the front seat and jerked the steering wheel away from the undead pedestrians.

"No!" Zack tried to the hit the brake but missed, flooring the gas pedal instead. The car sped, careening off the boulevard. They flew forward in their seats as the Cadillac smashed dead center into a lamppost.

"Everybody okay?" Zack asked, wedged between the windshield and the dashboard.

"No thanks to you." Zoe rolled her eyes and opened the side door.

"We're all good." Ozzie looked out the back window as the zombie parade craned their necks toward the accident. "Let's roll," he said, helping Zack off the dash of the totaled car.

"Thanks, Oz," Zack stuck the newspaper and the road map in his pocket as everyone took off, racing away from the undead madness.

CHAPTER

When they reached the used-car lot, the front gates were padlocked. "Just gimme a second." Ozzie pulled out a pair of wire-cutters from his pack and clipped out a corner of the chain link.

Madison lifted the fence away from the metal post, while everyone slid under to the other side.

Across the lot, an RV sat parked in the shadows—a Winnebago with bullhorns lashed to the grill front.

"That's what I'm talkin' about!" Zack ran over and opened the side door.

Rice stepped in first and flicked on a light. There was a fridge, microwave, bathroom, shower, bunk beds, two leather twirly chairs, and a breakfast nook. It was off the hook.

"This," Rice said slowly, "is our destiny."

"What is?" Madison asked, eyeing the RV with disgust. "Bed bugs?"

"Hey," Rice said, staring at Madison's wrist. "Where's your tracking bracelet?"

"A zombie ripped it off . . ." Her voice trailed to silence.

"Ah, man!" Rice moaned. "How's the prez gonna find us now?"

"Looks like we're officially on our own," Ozzie said.

"It's all good, guys." Zack threw down the newspaper article. "Check this out."

Rice and Zoe leaned over the breakfast table, reading the story.

"The evil genius of BurgerDog," Rice said with a hint of wonder in his voice. "What's the plan, Zacky boy?"

Zack spread the road map open now. "We gotta get from here to here." He dragged his pointer finger from Memphis, where they were, all the way west to Montana.

"Awesome plan." Zoe rolled her eyes skeptically.

"Wait, what's in Montana?" asked Ozzie.

"Here," said Rice, tossing Ozzie the newspaper.

"We can't drive to Montana," Zoe said. "We'll never make it!"

"We made it this far, didn't we?" said Rice.

"Yeah, when we had a freakin' airplane or a helicopter," Zoe argued. "And when Ozzie's leg wasn't broken."

"You guys, we have to find this guy!" Zack pleaded. "He's the only one who can help us."

"Okay, but . . ." Rice thought for a second while Ozzie and Madison finished reading the BurgerDog article. "Maybe this Duplessis guy won't want to help us. Maybe he just wants to zombify everything for, like, world domination. Or maybe it's a mind-control experiment gone horribly wrong. Or maybe he's trying to create an army of—"

"It doesn't matter," Ozzie interrupted. "This guy's got a high-tech lab, so either he's gonna help us out, or we're gonna bust him up. End of story."

Just then, a hulking, shadowy figure darkened the doorway. The faceless voice bellowed in a Southern twang. "She's a beaut, ain't she?"

"Hey!" Zack swung around. "Where the heck did you come from?"

"Suppose I might ask you the same dog garn question," the big man said and stepped into the light. He stood about six foot four and was dressed hideously—red-and-yellow checkered pants, a light blue corduroy sport coat over a pink button-down with a wide collar. A twisted tangle of gold chains dangled around his thick flabby neck. "Name's Leon Swanberg." The used-car salesman stuck out his hand. "Looks like you're in the market for a vee-hickle. Am I right or am I right?"

"Right you are, sir," Rice shook the man's hand. "We'd like to borrow this Winnebago, please."

"Borrow?" A frown fell over the salesman's face.

"You know, kind of like a loaner."

"I don't think so, kid. Cash is king, and I'm King of Cash. Just lendin' stuff out for free . . ." He shuddered. "Don't seem natural."

"Mr. Swanberg, we really need this RV," Zack pleaded.

"For what exactly?"

"So we can unzombify everybody and save the world, duh . . . ," Madison said.

"Unzomblify?" The salesman looked at them dubiously. "Is that a fact?"

"We have the anti—" Zoe started to say, but Zack silenced her with an elbow to the ribs. "Ow!" Zoe grabbed her side.

"We just need it," Zack said. "That's all."

Big Leon grabbed his chin and thought for a moment. "I can let y'all take the Winnie for oh, say, ten thou." He puckered his lips and nodded.

"Ten grand," Zoe scoffed. "Give us a break!"

"Tell ya what, I'll even throw in a copy of the yellow pages . . . so y'all can see over the steering wheel." Swanberg let out a beefy chuckle.

He was the only one laughing.

"We'll bring it back when we're done," Madison promised.

"It's a lose-lose for me, dontcha git it? Chances are you are all gonna get eaten by those zombie suckers, in which case I ain't never gonna see my car agee-in. Or now say you do unzomblicate everybody . . ."

"Unzombi*fy*," Rice corrected.

"Don't talk when I'm talkin', boy!" the salesman snapped. "My point is either way I ain't never gonna get compensated for this here fine vee-hickle." He slapped the tin siding of the Winnebago and left a dent. "If y'all save the world, yins probably be on the cover of magazines, gittin' spots on all the late-night talk shows, and y'all'll forget all about old Leon Swanberg, who gave yee the necessary means to accomplish your mission."

"Fine, if we get famous, we'll pay you," Zack said. "And we won't get eaten."

"That's what they all say." Old Leon's face went rigid. "I need a guarantee."

"Listen, Mister," Ozzie said. "We're guaranteed by

the executive branch of the United States government, and you, sir, are in direct violation of numerous federal statutes."

"Nice try, kid" He pushed the little army brat away. "But you can't con a con man. Now if you're not gonna make a purchase, then I'll have to ask you to leave."

"Fine!" Zoe dug through her mom's purse. "But all we have are credit cards."

"Well, why didn't you say so, little lady?" His voice perked up. "Lemme go draw up the paperwork and this puppy is all yours."

"Here." Zoe handed him Mrs. Clarke's American Express card.

"Don't leave home without it." The plaid-panted sleazebag took the credit card and strolled off toward his office.

"Zoe!" Zack strained in a low voice. "We can't buy a car!"

"Why not?" she said.

"Mom's gonna kill us!" he said.

"Mom's a zombie, Zack. She was gonna kill us anyway."

A few minutes later, Swanberg returned holding a bunch of contract papers. Zack winced and cosigned his name next to Zoe's. "Pleasure doing business with you." The salesman said, handing over the keys.

"Yeah, thanks," said Zack. He swiped the keychain while Rice and Ozzie began to load the jugs of gasoline into the compartment beneath the cargo hold.

Mr. Swanberg opened the gate, smiling.

What a jerk, Zack thought as they pulled out into the zombified night.

CHAPTER 7

The Winnebago sped over a long, flat bridge spanning a wide river, driving into downtown Memphis. On the sidewalk, a black crow perched on a decapitated zombie head and nipped at the undead meat with its beak.

Ozzie swung a right onto Beale Street, and they coasted under a gigantic neon guitar outside a blues club and past a skull-and-crossbones hanging above a voodoo souvenir shop. Both signs buzzed and flickered in the darkness. A few scattered zombies roamed the streets, barely noticing the RV shuttling through the city.

A short while later, the Winnebago made a wide left turn onto Elvis Presley Boulevard and passed a sign for Graceland. Up ahead a small shopping mart came into view, and Ozzie steered the Winnebago into its parking lot. "All right, guys," he said. "Lets stock up quick and get back on the road."

They hopped out of the Winnebago and moved toward the entrance in silence. Zack noticed a Holiday Inn set back from the road. The billboard out front read WELCOME TO ELVIS WEEK!

In front of the store, Rice pulled on the doors, but they were locked. Zack cupped his hands on the

glass and peeked inside. The place was deserted, the inventory untouched.

Zoe picked up a brick lying at the side of the building. "Looks like we're gonna have to do this the old-fashioned way." She raised her arm to throw, but Madison caught her by the wrist.

"Simmer down, Zoe." Madison walked up to the door and *pushed* on the handle. The door opened, jingling the welcome bell. She cocked an eyebrow and smirked. "Come on, dummies."

Once inside the store, Zoe and Madison went straight for the bath and body section to pick out some cosmetics. Rice walked down the snack aisle sweeping items into a basket. "Chips, soda, gummy worms, Cheez-Its, raisins for Madison, chips for moi." He then wandered over to a Halloween display, investigating all the weird costumes and gigantic bags of candy.

Zack's stomach growled. It was the first time since this whole thing began that he was actually hungry. At his feet, Twinkles panted, tongue hanging out. Someone else was hungry, too. Zack took a can of fancy dog food off the shelf and pulled back the tab. He set the puppy chow on the ground and petted Twinkles as the tiny pooch feasted away.

"Rice, get me some of those peanut butter M&Ms," Zack called out, walking down an aisle. "And some Sour Patch Kids."

Nobody responded. "Rice," Zack said loudly.

Still, no answer.

"Guys?" Zack called out, getting nervous.

Silence, then laughter.

"This isn't funny!"

Then Zoe's voice rang out. "There's a special on chill pills, little bro . . . You should pick some up for yourself."

"Thanks," Zack shouted back. "I'll get you a two-liter bottle of shut the heck up while I'm at it."

Then as he turned the corner at the end of the aisle, something jumped out in front of him.

"Rarrrrgh!"

"Ahhhh!" Zack leaped back into a soup-can pyramid, knocking the display to the floor.

Rice laughed, pulling off a zombie Halloween mask.

"Stop doing that!"

"Sorry." Rice shrugged. "I can't help it sometimes."

"Come on, children," Ozzie said one row over. "Quit messing around."

Zack and Rice turned down the next aisle, where Ozzie was grabbing two boxes of protein bars and a couple of Gatorades. "Ready?"

By the end of the supermarket sweep, their shopping baskets overflowed with every road-trip necessity imaginable: snacks and drinks, candy, toilet paper, disinfectant, batteries, paper towels, more snacks, toothbrushes, toothpaste, flashlights, water jugs, rubber gloves, plates, napkins, plastic forks and knives, travel-size board games, a deck of cards, CDs, electronics, DVDs, celebrity magazines, lip gloss, the Halloween mask, and, perhaps most important, Febreze.

When the boys walked to the front, Madison and Zoe were over by the register, scanning their items one by one.

"What are you doing?" Rice gave the girls a weird look.

Zoe punched in the total to the credit card machine and swiped the card in the reader. "Checking ourselves out. Duh!"

Zack rolled his eyes. "What else is new?"

As the girls bagged up the last of their goodies, a limping figure barged inside through the front door, clutching at the air. *"Raaaaaaaargh!"*

The zombie man wore a tight white jumpsuit with a bald eagle bedazzled on the front. Thick curly chest hair spilled out of the V-neck, all matted with sludge.

"OMG," said Madison. "Somebody call the fashion police."

Zoe picked up a soup can, wound up like a major league pitcher, and hocked a fastball at the zombie freak's noggin.

WHAM! The zombified weirdo dropped to the floor.

"Strike one!"

"Nice shot!" Madison high-fived her friend.

Rice walked over to the fallen zombie and studied its funny-looking costume, the oversize sunglasses, slick black hair, and swooping sideburns. "Elvis imper- sonator," he concluded. "Cool."

"Not cool!" Zack glanced out the storefront, where a large gang of zombies obstructed their path to the RV and now threatened to block their only exit.

"Come on!" shouted Ozzie, and they hauled

their booty outside, navigating through the broken doorway.

A dozen big jowly men with sideburns and thick chest fur gawked at them with lazy-eyed sneers. Some rocked big sparkly sunglasses with cracked lenses. Others wore red-and-gold capes. They all wore the same blank, dark liquid stare.

"Elvis convention . . ." Rice's eyes went wide with delight. "Sick."

The zombie Elvises plodded toward them like a goal line defense, frothing at the mouth, twitching vigorously with each rigorous step.

One of the Elvis lookalikes veered forward, grunting and grinding with a pelvis-led shimmy. Zack tried to sprint away, but the ghoulish freak lunged forward and took him by the elbow.

"Ouch! Let go!" Zack yanked his arm back as hard as he could, but the undead Elvis impersonator hung tight with a firm grip, panting at Zack, who kept pulling. The man's meaty hand wouldn't let go.

CHOMP!

The zombie clamped its scraggly brown teeth into Zack's forearm.

A sharp volt of pain shot through Zack's chest as the ravenous glutton tore into his skin like a turkey drumstick.

"It's eating me!" Zack screamed and ripped his arm away, as the Elvis lookalike chewed the armflesh with its mouth open.

Nom nom nom . . .

Zack staggered back and fell to the pavement in a daze of pain and shock.

The beady-eyed beast thrust its jaw forward and lunged at Zack for a second helping. Zack clambered to his feet, clutching his arm. He spotted a clear lane to the Winnebago and went for it. *WHAM!* He slammed into a wall of polyester as another zombie Elvis hip-checked him back to the ground with a sidelong pelvic thrust. Zack's head bashed back on the cement and his eyes flashed red.

"Hoobity-hoobla!" The Elvis zombie raised its claws, and Zack could hear his own heart thumping as he

cowered on the blacktop. He shielded his eyes with his bleeding arm, steeling himself for the zombie's death clamp. But none came. Instead, something heavy plopped beside him on the ground.

Zack's eyes popped open to see the zombie galoot splayed out on the pavement. Ozzie Briggs stood over him, blowing imaginary gun smoke off the rubber end of his crutch.

"Come on, slowpoke!" Zoe yanked her brother's good arm and pulled him to his feet. "Giddyup!" Zack half-ran, half-fell as she dragged him away from the undead lounge lizards and toward the Winnebago. Ozzie galloped on his crutches and plopped into the driver's seat next to Madison, riding shotgun with Twinkles. Zack and Zoe dove in the getaway ride, and Rice slammed the door.

Zack collapsed on his back while the swarm of undead Elvis wannabes pummeled the sides of the Winnebago with their fists.

Boom! Bang! Whap!

"Go!" Madison yelled, and Ozzie hit the gas.

The engine vroomed, and the rear tires spun up smoke as they peeled out screeching into the bloodred dawn.

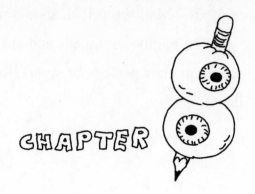

CHAPTER 8

Twinkles slipped off Madison's lap and trotted back to Zack, lying wounded on the bottom bunk. The little puppy jumped up on Zack's chest and touched his face with its paw. As they shuttled up the highway, Madison turned on the radio and tuned the knob through the stations. There was nothing but static on every channel. The national Emergency Alert System had long since given up.

"Ugh." Madison pouted. "I just want to hear some music . . ."

Zack's arm throbbed, searing with pain, and he bit his lip as Rice tended to his zombie bite. Rice was humming a little ditty when he suddenly broke into song. "You ate nothin' but a BurgerDog . . . growlin' all the time." It was his made-up version of an Elvis classic. "You ate nothin' but a BurgerDog . . . all covered in slime." Zack glared at his friend, wishing he would stop singing.

"You ain't never caught a Chaser, but you bit a friend of mine." He smiled and did his best Elvis imitation. "Thank you very much."

"I don't think she was talking about that kind of music, Rice," Ozzie said.

"Ew." Zoe leaned down from the top bunk. "He isn't going to turn into a zombie again, is he?"

"Yup," Zack said. "And then I'm going to eat your face off."

Zoe punched her fist into her hand and snorted. "I don't think so."

Zack wondered if he might really turn back into a zombie. He didn't feel sick yet. Despite the pain in his arm, he felt fine, actually. But he didn't know for sure if he would rezombify. Madison couldn't, but that was

Madison. She couldn't zombify at all. Zoe hadn't been rebitten yet, so there was no way to really know.

Rice finished wrapping the gauze and looked at Zack. "Tell me if this hurts." He jabbed his index finger into the bandaged-up bite wound.

"Ow!" Zack yelped. "Dude!"

"You'll be fine." Rice patted Zack's head. "Just get some rest." Then he called to Ozzie in the front of the Winnebago. "Hey, Oz, so, like, we're the only two left who can turn into zombies . . . Isn't that cool?"

"Yeah," Ozzie replied, keeping his eye on the road. "Totally." He weaved the Winnebago through an obstacle course of undead flesh-eaters cluttering up the highway.

Zack could hear their subhuman moaning over the hum of the motor. He pulled the window curtain to the side and stared out at the interstate, watching the trees whiz by silently. The sun blazed brightly in the clear blue sky as they sped along the northbound highway up the east bank of the Mississippi River. An infinity of zombies stumbled over the rolling hillsides, casting long shadows in the morning light.

Same nightmare. Different day.

Madison and Zoe rolled down the windows as the road opened up and the zombies grew sparser. The air was crisp, whisking in from the cool morning. They rode on for some time in silence. Things were almost peaceful for a while, and Zack's mind started to drift.

Then out of nowhere, the Winnebago slowed to a halt. A sickening scent wafted in through the open windows, and everything reeked of old toe jam. Madison covered her mouth and sprayed Febreze air freshener.

"Why are we stopping?" Zack asked, covering his mouth. "It stinks!" He stuck his head between the front seats and peered through the windshield.

A cloudy sky loomed over the Mississippi, and distant lightning pulsed behind the pine-clad hills on the western horizon. In front of them, a massive traffic jam clogged up the bridge the entire way across. Dozens of zombies lumbered through the gridlock.

They had no choice but to turn around. Rice studied the map intently now. "Keep going north, and we can cross at this other bridge."

"Roger dodger, Rice-man." Ozzie shifted gears and reversed the RV down the sloped pavement back the way they came.

"Rice, are you sure you know where you're going?" Zack asked.

"Don't worry, buddy. We'll be there in no time."

While they wended their way through the small-town streets of Collinsville, Illinois, Madison and Zoe sat in the back, painting their nails at the breakfast table.

"You better not have gotten us lost, my little dorkling," said Zoe.

"Almost there," Rice said, glancing down at the map.

As the Winnebago climbed the upward slope of the road, an enormous catsup bottle rose majestically out of the not-too-distant foliage.

"Whoaaaa," Rice said slack-jawed. "There it is!"

"What the heck is that?" Ozzie hit the brakes gently, and they came to a stop on the lip of the hill.

"That, my friend," Rice revealed, "is the World's Largest Catsup Bottle."

Madison and Zoe gazed through the slats in the window blinds. "I think he meant 'What the heck are we doing here?'"

"Okay, A, it's awesome," Rice said. "And B, my Uncle Ben is from around here, and he told me once that a man hasn't lived until he's seen the Catsup Bottle firsthand."

"C," Madison said, "you're a huge weirdo."

Rice ignored her snide remark. "Do you think it's really filled with catsup?"

"That would be crazy," said Zack. "Where would they get it all?"

"It's a water tower, dorkbrains." Zoe sighed.

"Come on, let's go check it out," Ozzie looked back at the girls. "You comin'?"

Madison blew on her nails. "I think we'll pass."

"Suit yourselves," Rice said and jumped down to the pavement.

The boys got out and took turns looking through Ozzie's binoculars at the giant catsup bottle standing tall against the cloud-curtained sky.

Rice was mesmerized.

A sharp wind whisked in their faces, and a dark menacing cloudbank rumbled. The late morning sky tinged a greenish color. A chilly chill shot down Zack's spine.

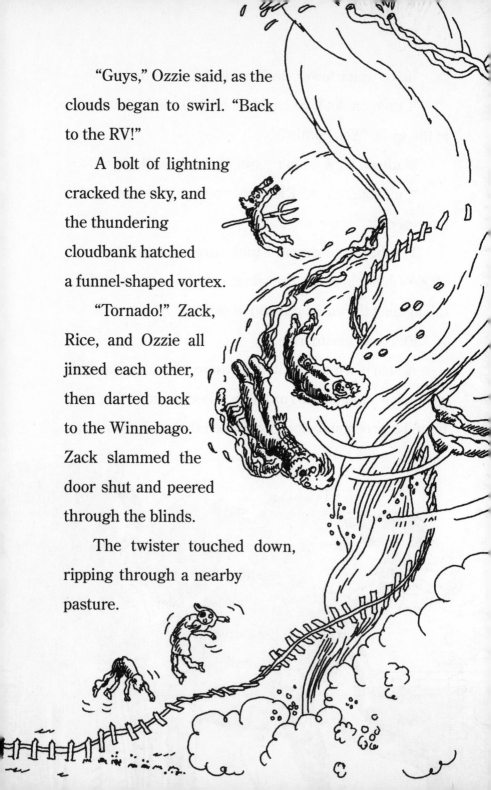

"Guys," Ozzie said, as the clouds began to swirl. "Back to the RV!"

A bolt of lightning cracked the sky, and the thundering cloudbank hatched a funnel-shaped vortex.

"Tornado!" Zack, Rice, and Ozzie all jinxed each other, then darted back to the Winnebago. Zack slammed the door shut and peered through the blinds.

The twister touched down, ripping through a nearby pasture.

The swirling pillar of black wind was headed straight toward them, whipping up zombies in a slow-motion swirl.

"We have to find a basement," Rice said.

"You're right," Zack agreed. "People always go in basements."

"What people?" Madison asked, trying to soothe her very freaked-out puppy.

"Movie people," Rice said.

Through the windshield, Ozzie surveyed the landscape with the binoculars. "Down there!" He pointed his finger toward the base of the hill.

"A basement?" Zack took the binoculars from Ozzie. At the end of the road was a short tunnel running under a railway overpass. "Let's go!" Zack yelled.

Zoe jumped behind the wheel and started the RV. Buckets of hail and sleet pelted the roof of the Winnebago as she zoomed down the slickening black asphalt.

Phlooosshhhhhhhhhh!

They whizzed around a bend, and Zoe floored the pedal, swerving around a green-and-yellow tractor that floated through the air. Splintered planks of wood and cinder blocks soared around in the zero-gravity wind.

Zoe steered clear of a huge piece of sheet metal rattling across the street, and the Winnebago shot under the overpass. She slammed on the brakes and shut off the engine. The daylight darkened in the eye of the storm as the whirlwind spun over the tunnel. Zoe flipped on the headlights.

The zombified townsfolk flew in from both sides, torpedoing through the air. A crankle-faced farmer in denim overalls clung upside down to the windshield, leaving a sludgy smear as it pinwheeled on the glass and flew over the roof.

"Aaaack!" Madison squealed. A mutilated arm

smashed through the window above the sink, groping and snatching blindly.

The zombie wedged its mangled head in, cracking the window frame. Its festering skin scraped off in hideous gray clumps on the jagged glass.

Rice screamed like a girl in a horror movie.

Zack held one of Ozzie's crutches like a bayonet and jabbed the shrieking fiend in the face until it popped out of the window.

"Zoe, start the engine!" Ozzie shouted while more zombies belted into the side panels, denting the roof and busting up the windows.

But then the wind abated, and the airborne zombies dropped to the pavement around the RV. The wind-tunnel zombies rose off the road, grunting like a hungry pack of wild simians, and converged on the Winnebago.

"It won't start!" Zoe screamed, cranking the key. The engine sputtered over like a broken record and finally wheezed out.

Just then, a massive cracking sound pierced the air.

"What the heck was that?" asked Zack.

Ahead of them, through the tunnel's exit, something toppled—something big—and within seconds, a tide of water rushed under the overpass and swept the zombie horde away.

"Now," said Zack. "Go!"

Zoe turned the key again and pumped the accelerator.

The engine revved. She hit the gas, and they zoomed out of the tunnel away from the zombies beached on the asphalt. They swerved through the demolished wreckage of the World's Largest Catsup Bottle and watched the tornado dissipate into thin air.

"Hey, guys," Zack said once they were back on the highway. "No more pit stops, okay?" No one answered him. He was exhausted. They all were. Zack closed his eyes and fell abruptly asleep.

CHAPTER

"**A**lmost there, Mad!" Zack woke up to the sound of his sister's voice. Bewildered and groggy, he looked at the time. The digital clock on the dashboard glowed faintly in the growing dark: 7:23 P.M.

"Hey there, Mr. Sleepyhead," said Zoe.

"Where are we almost?" Zack asked.

"The Mall of America," she said matter-of-factly.

"We've lost enough time already!" Zack said. "We're not going to a stupid mall."

"We're not going to a stupid mall," she agreed. "We're going to an awesome mall!"

"No, we're not," Zack whined.

"Listen, little bro," Zoe cocked her head to the side and gave him a look that meant business. "I've been driving for the past nine hours, and we'll go where I say we'll go. Capische?"

"But we're supposed to be going straight to Montana," Zack pleaded. "I thought we all agreed."

"Zip it, Zacky-poo," said Zoe.

"Zoe, Mom and Dad's eyeballs could be falling out right now, and all you care about is going shopping? Where's Rice?"

"Taking a shower," Madison informed him.

Over the roar of the motor, Zack could hear his buddy whistling in the bathroom. *The sun'll come out to-morrow . . .*

"Does he know we're going to the Mall of America?"

"Are you kidding?" Zoe answered. "It was his idea."

"Rice!" Zack hollered, but his buddy kept on whistling away.

"OMG, Zo," Madison exclaimed. "I can't wait to get out of these clothes. I've been wearing the same thing since, like, forever ago."

"I know," Zoe said. "It's, like, completely horrifying."

"Wait a sec . . ." Zack kept up his protest. "Ozzie?"

Ozzie's arm was hanging off the top bunk. He snored loudly, snoozing deeply. Zack grunted. The girls had officially taken over.

Rice waltzed out of the Winnebago bathroom with a towel wrapped around his waist and another one draped over his shoulders. "It's cool, buddy," he said to Zack. "If we're going to battle Duplessis and his army of ghouls, we're gonna need some serious equipment upgrades."

"Yeah, Zack," Madison added. "And we'll all get clean clothes and new shoes and makeup and maybe even Jamba Juices."

"Fine!" Zack crossed his arms over his chest. He *hated* going to malls.

Just then Zoe caught a glimpse of Rice in the rearview. "Ew. Put a shirt on."

A short while later, the Winnebago turned into the parking lot of the Mall of America. Outside the main entrance, Zoe eased off the accelerator and killed the engine. They left the RV and strolled to the entrance of the gargantuan shopping center.

The glass doors slid open automatically, and a horrific stench seeped out in a warm puff, like air-conditioning on a hot day. The mall was brightly lit, sickeningly fluorescent. The stores flanking either side of the arcade were completely demolished—glass smashed, clothing racks toppled, shelving units torn down and products strewn everywhere. Except for that and the phlegm-gurgling moan of the undead reverberating through the whole place, it looked like a typical shopping day: people milling around zombielike from store to store.

Something scuttled by their feet. Zack squinted at the shapeless form undulating quickly across the linoleum.

"Ah!" Madison shrieked. Suddenly a slime-soaked leopard-skin coat leaped off the ground like a rabid flying squirrel and latched onto her face, muffling her horrified yowl. She pulled the zombified fur coat off her face and flung it to the floor.

Twinkles yapped, but not at the furrier's nightmare. Walking on its fingertips, a severed hand sniffed around caninelike with its middle finger. Twinkles bared his teeth and purred with a vicious growl.

"Come on, boy!" Zack called to the pup, and Twinkles followed along.

An undead hobo lady wearing a long coat and wool cap took a painful step forward as the kids passed her by. She cocked her head, mewling like a dumb cat, then bared her gnarly rotten teeth and hissed.

As they crept deeper through the galleria, they

came to a roller coaster corkscrewing up the four-story atrium at the center of the complex.

"No way we're waiting in this line!" Madison crossed her arms and glared at the undead ranks rampaging behind the gates of the amusement park.

Zombie parents swayed, baby-stepping around like giant toddlers. Their zombie rug rats crawled about on all fours, barking and snarling. There were zombies climbing up the Ferris wheel and flying off the tilt-a-whirl into the branches of the indoor trees that sprouted out of the linoleum floor.

"Maybe this wasn't such

a good idea, guys," Zack said, gazing around. "Let's go. We can pick up stuff somewhere else."

"No, wait," Madison said. "There are no zombies up there!" She pointed above them to the second floor, which appeared to be uninfested.

"We've got to get up there!" Zoe ran to the mall directory and checked the map. "That way!" She pointed down a corridor where a dense pack of five-foot-tall zombies blocked their way. A creepy-eyed army of undead clones trudged steadily toward them: pigtailed zweenybopper Children of the Damned.

"Where did the Jonas Brothers fan club come from?" Ozzie gulped.

"More like the Groanas Brothers," Rice quipped.

The undead preteens stamped forward. More zombies started to close in as if guided by radar, and the five of them retreated to the alcove by the restrooms. Zack glanced around the corner and spotted a cardboard cutout of Justin Bieber standing outside a record store. "I have an idea." He sprinted over to the life-size Bieber and placed it away from where they needed to go.

"Zack," Rice called in a whisper. "Get back here, what are you doing?"

Zack hid behind the cardboard Bieber cutout and, despite his embarrassment, launched into his finest rendition of the pop singer's hit song, "Baby."

The zweenyboppers twizzled their necks toward the sound of Zack's sweet falsetto voice. "Baby, baby, baby, oh!"

The Bieber-maniacs stampeded toward Zack's singing. He jumped out from behind the life-size cutout and sprinted around the pack of zombie girls as they tore the pop-star decoy to bits.

"Wow, Zack," Rice ribbed him. "Didn't know you were such a fan of the Biebs."

Zack shrugged, and they made a break down the hallway, away from the undead swarm. They hung a right by a jewelry kiosk and stopped in front of the elevators. Madison hit the call button and the doors opened. Inside the car lift, Zoe pressed the button for the fourth floor. Zack pressed the one for level two.

"What are you doing?" Zoe asked him.

"We're going to the sporting goods store."

"Well, *we're* going to Bloomingdale's." Madison hooked arms with Zoe.

"That's right, dweebo," said Zoe.

"Fine," Zack said. "We'll meet right here in one hour."

"Are you kidding me?" Madison whined. "That's barely enough time to pick out a pair of shoes. "

The doors opened again, and the boys got out on the second floor.

Twinkles trotted forward.

"Hey, look," said Rice. "He wants to come with the boys."

"Twinkles, stay!" Madison ordered her pup. Twinkles stopped between the closing doors.

"Twinkles . . . come!" Zack called, slapping his knee.

"Stay!" Madison commanded.

"Twinkles, come to the one you love best!" Zack called again.

"Twinkles does not love *you* best." Madison narrowed her eyes. "Twinkles, stay!"

"Come on, boy!" Ozzie urged the confused puppy.

"Guys, knock it off!" demanded Zoe. "Twinkles is coming with us." The doors started to close, and Twinkles hopped back in the elevator.

"Ha!" Madison scooped up her pup.

"One hour." Zack stuck his arm between the doors, and they reopened. "Seriously."

"We'll think about it," Zoe said, hitting the button repeatedly. "Seriously."

The elevator shut, and the boys turned to look at one another.

Rice stood between Zack and Ozzie and clasped both of their shoulders. "I'm glad we're dudes," he said.

"Seriously," Ozzie and Zack said together, and they walked off through the empty second level. Clear and zombie-free.

CHAPTER

The boys strolled inside the sporting goods store and checked out the footwear on the wall of sneakers. They picked out some fresh kicks and new gear from the clothes racks: T-shirts, windpants, sweatshirts, and blessedly clean socks.

"What can I make with you?" Rice stretched a long tube sock end to end, eyeing a display bin full of baseballs. He walked over and dropped three of the balls into the toe of the soccer sock. He tied off the end with a knot and swung the makeshift bludgeon slowly. "Cool!" He smiled.

"Nice, Rice," Ozzie said. "Let me show you

something." He grabbed his new pupil by the wrist and adjusted his grip.

"Yes, sensei." Rice bowed respectfully to Ozzie as the lesson began.

"I'll be back in a minute." Zack grabbed a shopping cart and pushed it through the aisles. The shelves were stacked high with everything from volleyballs to fishing poles. He picked out a couple of baseball bats, a few lacrosse sticks, and a bunch of unstrung tennis rackets. He went on tipping items into the belly of the cart, anything that looked useful: boxing gloves, lacrosse gear, elbow pads, and football helmets. Before he knew it, the cart was almost full.

"Come on, Zack," Ozzie called over.

"We got to hit up a couple more stores," said Rice. "I want to pick up a little TV for the Winnie and get a new iPhone."

Out in the mall corridor, they peered over the railing into the pit of zombies stumbling around below. On the first level, all the escalators were running downward, confining the undead savages to the ground floor.

"Let's keep moving," Zack said over the roar of the zombie moans.

When they reached the next storefront, the lights were off. Zack squinted through the metal pull-down grate, when a zombie hand slapped the inside door with a loud *thump*, breaking the silence. Zack flinched and peered in again. The undead palm had smeared a handprint down the interior glass. The store was jam-packed with undead mall-goers, contorted bodies crammed together like a subway car at rush hour. The zombies writhed like a slow-motion mosh pit.

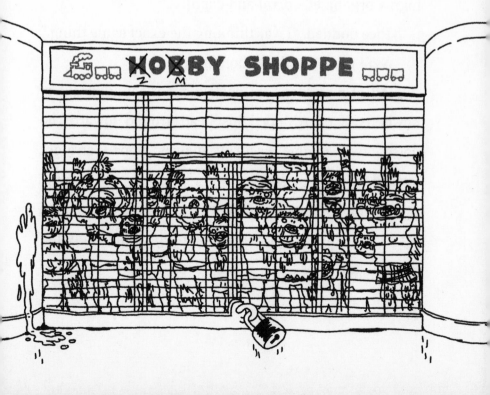

"Bummer, man," Zack said to Rice. "It's all filled up with zombies."

Ozzie peered over the railing again at the living dead moving too slowly to make any progress up the escalator treadmill.

"I don't get it," Zack said. "How come there's only zombies down there and locked in the stores?"

Ozzie gazed into the distance. "Someone else is here."

"Yeah, a butt-load of zombies," Rice said.

"No, I mean somebody with a brain," Ozzie continued. "This looks like a tactical sweep and lockdown, a highly organized corral-and-capture."

Rice nodded. "I was thinking the exact same thing."

Sure you were, Zack thought.

All of a sudden, an electric zoom sounded out of nowhere. Zack whipped his head around toward the noise. Two zombie security guards zipped straight toward them on Segways.

"Ahhh! Get down." Zack hit the deck as the undead mall cops leaped off their scooters, tackling Rice and Ozzie to the floor.

"Hey!" Rice ripped off the security guard's black clip-on tie. "You're not even a real cop!"

Zack grabbed one of the tennis rackets and brought it down over the zombie's head, collaring it around the

neck. He yanked back hard and dragged the zombie off Rice before the undead mall cop could bite down on his best friend. The zombie flailed its arm like a club, grazing Zack's chin. It whirled around so they were nose-to-nose and sneezed, blasting Zack right in the face with infectious snot. Zack winced.

The undead security guard roared and twisted its torso, then body-slammed Zack onto the linoleum floor. The zombie rose to its feet and seized Zack by the ankle, hoisting him upside-down off the floor. "Yow!" Zack kicked his leg to break free, but the mall cop's grip was too firm. The zombie was mere inches away from nibbling Zack's Achilles tendon. "Help!" Zack yelled.

"I gotcha, buddy!" Rice picked up the soccer sock stuffed with baseballs from the cart, took a few running steps, and clobbered the zombie with one deft crack of his wrist. The zombie keeled over, and Zack fell on his head next to the unconscious goon lying beside him.

"Thanks, buddy." Zack stood up and brushed himself off. "Nice moves, by the way."

"Little help over here, please," Ozzie called, his

back to the floor, bench-pressing the other crazed mall cop with his crutch. "This guy's heavy." Rice spun on his heel, wielding the bootleg weapon, and crowned the second zombie with a whap.

"Wah . . . wah." Rice made kung-fu noises.

Ozzie jumped to his feet, balancing on his good leg. "Excellent technique, Rice. We'll need to work on your reaction time, though." He clapped the slime off his hands.

"No problem, dude," Rice said, karate-chopping the air with the edge of his hand.

Ozzie smirked and then hobbled over to one of the discarded Segways. He propped it up and hopped on. Then he zipped forward, stopped, did a little turn, then whizzed forward again in a big looping figure eight.

Zack and Rice stared at the other Segway, then looked at each other. "On your mark . . . ," Rice said.

"Get set . . . ," said Zack, bending one knee.

Rice took off early, bolting for the other Segway. "Go!"

"Cheater!" Zack broke into a sprint and caught up to his buddy, who was chugging as fast as he could. Suddenly, Rice slipped on some slime and fell flat on his back. Zack caught up quickly and took the lead.

"Ooooh!" Rice winced in pain, rolling onto his tummy.

Zack stopped midway to the Segway and looked

back at Rice, grabbing at his tailbone, his face scrunched in agony. He jogged back over and helped Rice to his feet. "You okay, man?" he asked.

A devilish grin flashed across Rice's face, and he took off again for the Segway, perfectly fine.

"No fair, man!" Zack shouted as his friend hopped on the two-wheeled scooter and rode up to him. Rice leaned forward stiffly on the Segway speaking in a robot voice. "I am from the planet Zorgone, me and my army of slug larvae are going to take over your brains for undisclosed purposes . . ."

"Five minutes, then it's my turn." Zack laughed at his friend. "Okay?"

"Ten minutes," Rice called back, zipping off after Ozzie.

"We only have fifteen before we have to meet back up with the girls."

Zack walked over to the conked-out mall cops. Their motionless bodies were sprawled out on the floor like crime-scene chalk outlines. Zack cautiously nudged one of them with his toe. The unconscious zombie jiggled a little and then fell still. He examined their cheap plastic badges, their starchy white polyester shirts, and the walkie-talkies clipped to both of their collars.

Zack reached down slowly, snatched both of the two-way radios, and then dashed after Rice and Ozzie.

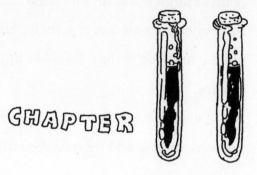

CHAPTER 11

ack at the elevators, Zack waited for the girls and toyed around with the security radios. He looked up at Rice and Ozzie, who were still scooting around on the deluxe Segways. "You know it's almost my turn, guys?"

"Yeah, yeah, we know!" Rice called back, racing after Ozzie.

Zack clicked the button on the two-way radio and spoke into the receiver. "Zaaack, I am your fa-ther . . ." His voice came out of the other speaker. Rice was right: He did sound a little whiny.

Just then, the elevator dinged, and the doors parted.

Madison and Zoe burst out of the car, all dressed up and reeking of perfume. Zoe wore fancy high heels, an expensive necklace, and a sleek black evening gown. Madison was decked out in designer leggings and a little waistcoat that made her look like a fashionable pirate. But despite their chic attire, the mean girls both looked nervous.

"What's the matter?" Zack asked, picking up on their panicky vibe.

"Um . . ." Zoe panted. "We're in trouble."

"But it's not our fault . . . ," Madison added, as Rice and Ozzie zipped over on the Segways. They slowed to a standstill and listened up.

"See, it all started when we were trying to find Twinkles a sweater, but we took a wrong turn and wound up in Home Furnishings, and then all of a sudden these two guys came out of nowhere, pushing a leather couch."

"And they were all like 'hey baby' this and 'hey baby' that," Zoe finished.

"What guys?" Rice asked confused.

"Really cute high-school guys with awesome haircuts just like Justin Bieber."

"High school?" asked Zack with a tone of disapproval.

"So, yeah," Madison continued. "Their names are Dustin and Frankie . . ."

"And then, like, we started talking to them," Zoe went on.

"Yeah, and when we told them about the antidote—"

"You told them about the antidote?" Rice screeched.

"I know it was stupid," Madison said. "Our B."

Zack smacked his forehead, flabbergasted.

"Anyways, they got all weird and sketchy and wanted it for themselves, like that little troll guy in *Lord of the Hobbits*."

"Exactly!" Madison agreed. "They were like dirty little Bieber hobbits!"

"And then those jerks kidnapped Twinkles and said if we didn't come back with the antidote in ten minutes . . . they're gonna feed the little mutt to their other friend, who's a zombie!"

"So then we told them Rice had it," Madison said.

"Why'd you do that for?" Rice winced. "Your bro's the one who has it."

"Huh?" Zack raised his eyebrows. "I thought you had it."

"Noooo," Rice said. "I specifically remember me giving it to you."

"I'm pretty sure," Zack patted his pockets with a concerned look on his face.

"Zack!" Rice shouted and riffled frantically through his backpack. "It's not here!"

"I'm just messing with you," Zack snickered and held up the vial.

"Not funny, dude!"

"Yeah, Zack," said Madison. "This isn't a joke. Twinkles's life is at stake."

"Well, what are we waiting for?" Ozzie asked. "Let's go get him back!"

"Okay, but we're not just handing over the antidote," said Rice.

"No way!" Zack said adamantly. "Just listen up. I got a plan. Come on." He marched briskly, leading them down the mall arcade and stopping in front of a toy store. The aisles were flooded with boxes and board games, action figure packages, and remote control helicopters.

"Remember that science kit Mom and Dad got me when I was little?"

"You were so happy." Zoe remembered. "That's how I knew you'd be a nerd."

"Why are we here?" Madison asked.

"We need another one of these." Zack held the antidote vial between his thumb and forefinger and stepped into the store.

They started digging through the landfill of toys, until Rice held up a flat rectangular box. "Jackpot!" He tore open the beginner science kit. There were beakers and test tubes and little packets of chemicals. Rice handed Zack one of the test tubes.

"What are we gonna fill it with?" he asked.

The World's Largest Catsup Bottle flashed through Zack's mind, and he led them all to a hotdog stand where

he mixed a little catsup with a dash of cola, and voilà! Zack poured the ruddy concoction into the toy vial, then held up the real antidote next to the fake one.

"Perfect," everyone agreed. The two test tubes were almost identical.

Now that they had the imitation serum, they had to figure out the best way to approach the teenage dognappers. Zack felt the weight of the security guard radios in his hands. *We have the Segways. And the "antidote."* "Hey, Madison," he said. "How many of us do they think we are?"

"We only mentioned Rice," she replied. "Not you or Ozzie."

"Good," he said. "I'm gonna be Rice."

"Hah!" Rice scoffed. "You don't have the chops!"

Zack eyed his pal skeptically and handed Ozzie the other mall cop's radio. "You two are gonna listen in and back us up." Zack wore his radio beneath his shirt like an undercover police wire.

"So wait, what's the plan again?" Madison asked.

"We're gonna go in and offer them a truce. If they don't take it, then we'll trade the fake antidote for Twinkles." He turned to his boys. "Then you two are gonna swoop in, and biggity-bam, we're off to the races."

"Biggity-bam, huh?" Zoe said, cocking an incredulous eyebrow.

"Okay, Zack," said Ozzie. "This could work, but remember, you gotta be cool."

"Hah!" Zoe scoffed. "Fat chance."

CHAPTER 12

oe pushed the shopping cart full of their new sporting equipment into the elevator with Zack and Madison. Zack gave the ready signal to his boys and hit the button for the fourth floor. Ozzie and Rice were to follow them up on their Segways in a separate elevator car.

Moments later, the doors parted on the uppermost level.

Zack's pulse was beating like a bongo drum as he stepped off the elevator. He checked his back pocket for the phony serum and followed his sister and Madison.

Walking through the top floor of the mall, they

passed by two camping tents set up outside the movie theater. Across from the box office, a zombified teenager was locked behind the cookie stand with the gate pulled down. The zombie gnashed its teeth on the steel metal grate, shaking the bars like an angry prisoner.

A little farther down, two tan leather easy chairs faced an enormous flat-screen TV set up in the middle of the hall. Between the two chairs, Twinkles whinnied and pawed weakly at the metal pet store cage holding him captive.

As they moved closer, Zack could see two pairs of hands gripping wireless Xbox controllers. They were playing *Flesh Feast 4*—the one video game Zack's parents would never let him play. The object of the game was to kill as many zombies as possible.

"Heard a rumor you guys were looking for me." Zack played it cool and held his breath in the silence that followed.

The two avatars on the screen froze and were quickly gobbled by the video-game zombies. Then the leather chairs spun around, and two fifteen-year-old boys stood up and tossed their controllers to the ground.

The boy on the right was long and lanky, a good six feet tall, maybe taller. He had bleach-blond hair meticulously messed up with an expertly coiffed swoosh over one of his eyes. His face was shrouded by a black hoodie with a skeleton's ribcage and pelvis printed on the front like an X-ray. The boy on the left was about six inches shorter than his counterpart, though still much bigger than Zack. His face was lean and angular, and his eyes were hidden behind a pair of sunglasses. He tipped his head down, peering over the rim of his shades and smiled.

"You must be Bryce," said the shorter one.

"Rice," Zack corrected him.

"I'm just gonna call you Dork for now."

"Rice the dork." The tall boy sneered.

"Yeah, well, what's your name?"

Zack could feel a cold trickle of sweat fall behind his ear. "We haven't been properly introduced."

"Name's Frankie, kid," the tall boy said. "Frankie McFadden."

"I'm Dustin," said the shorter one.

"Well, Dustin . . . Frankie," Zack addressed the diabolical duo. "We're here for Twinkles."

"What's a Twinkles?" Frankie asked.

"That's his name," Madison piped up, gesturing at the caged pup.

"No, it's not," Frankie balked. "His name is Brutus."

"As if . . ." Madison squealed. "It's Twinkles, now give him back!"

"Why don't you make me?"

"Everybody take it easy,"

Zack said calmly. "We're just talkin' here."

"We'll give you the dog back when you hand over the antidote," Dustin said.

Zack gulped and wiped his sweaty palms on his jeans. "If all you want to do is unzombify your friend over there . . ." He pointed to the kid stashed inside the cookie stand. "Then we're prepared to trade you one dose in exchange for the dog."

"That's not exactly what we had in mind." Dustin smiled evilly.

"Well, what *did* you have in mind?" Zoe asked.

"We haven't really decided yet, but the girl that works at the movie theater is super hot."

"Don't forget the chick who works at American Eagle—"

"Wait a second," Zack interrupted. "Your plan is to waste all the antidote on a few stupid girls? You're nuts."

"Allow me to explain something to you, Dork," Dustin said, cracking his neck. "Frankie and me don't care about saving everyone. We've got the Mall of

America all to ourselves. We could live here for years without ever having to leave. We've got big plans for this place, so like I said before, give us the potion, or the dog gets it . . ."

"Sorry, man." Zack held firm. "Can't do it."

"Then it's time to say good-bye to your little mutt," Dustin said, pulling Twinkles out of the cage.

"For the last freakin' time," Madison said. "Twinkles is *not* a mutt!"

"Come, come, Brutus." Dustin walked over to the cookie stand with their puppy. His zombified friend growled behind the pull-down grate. Dustin dangled the little dog by one paw and cackled. Twinkles squeaked and twisted helplessly over the zombie's hot slavering maw.

"Let go of my dog, you smelly little hipster!" Madison shrieked at the top of her lungs.

"Are you sure that's what you want me to do?" Dustin asked with mock concern. He lowered Twinkles a little closer to the chomping jaws of their slobbering zombie pal. Frankie laughed like a goof, clapping his

hands together and hopping from foot to foot.

"You two make me sick!" yelled Zoe, her nostrils flaring.

"Stop!" Madison pleaded, nearly bursting into tears.

"Ah, what?" Frankie jeered. "Baby gonna cry?"

Zack saw red, and before he knew what he was doing, he charged forward and grabbed Frankie around the waist, trying to tackle him to the ground. Zoe and Madison's jaws both dropped. "Zack, don't!"

"Bad move, phlegm-wad!"

Frankie picked Zack up with ease, spun him around like a small child and then slammed him down face-first onto the seat cushion. Frankie dug his knee into Zack's back and mushed his face into the leather seat. "Did I keep it warm enough for you?"

"Wait!" Madison winked at Zack. "You can have it. Just leave him alone."

"Yeah, Zack, it's not worth it," Zoe said now. "Just give it up and everything will be okay." She sounded like she was reading from a bad movie script.

Note to self, Zack thought. *My sister's a horrible actress.*

"Fine." Zack grunted and reached his arm back, pulling the tube of red liquid out of his pocket. "Here!" Frankie ripped the test tube out of Zack's hand.

"I see you've come to your senses." Dustin walked away from the cookie stand and flung Twinkles bouncing hard across the floor.

Madison gasped and picked up her puppy, glowering at Dustin.

Frankie shoved Zack down harshly and let go.

Dustin took the test tube from Frankie. He held the phony serum vial high in the air, grinning psychotically, a mad gleam twinkling in the mallrat's eyes.

CHAPTER

"All right," Zack said. "You got what you wanted." He turned to Madison and Zoe. "Let's get out of here . . ."

"Not so fast," Dustin interrupted. "Now we have to see if it actually works." He snapped his fingers, and Frankie grabbed Madison, restraining her with her arms behind her back. Twinkles dropped to the floor, yapping away.

"Ow, jerko," she cried. "Take it easy!"

"Let her go, dirtbag!" Zack demanded.

Dustin unscrewed the vial of antidote and walked back over to the cookie stand. He let a few drops fall on his undead friend's wriggling zombie tongue.

"Not too much, bro," said Frankie. "Save some for the babes."

"How long does this stuff take to kick in?" Dustin asked as their zombie friend gargled down the catsup-y concoction.

"Five minutes, tops," Zack replied, massaging the soreness out of his arm. "It depends."

"Well, it better work if you guys want to walk out of here with your brains intact." Dustin dragged a line across his throat with his finger. "Wait right there." Frankie tightened his grip on Madison as the bullies observed their "unzombifying" buddy with anticipation.

"Where are Rice and Ozzie?" Zoe asked her brother through clenched teeth.

Zack shrugged. They *should* have been here by now.

"That's one minute," Dustin announced, still staring at his watch.

Frankie glared at Zack suspiciously, holding Madison in a half nelson. Dustin sniffed the test tube, daubed a drop of it on his finger, and gave it a lick. He looked at Frankie and narrowed his eyes. "Catsup."

Dustin whipped his head around, wild-eyed with rage, and smashed the vial of phony antidote on the floor. Frankie grabbed Madison by the wrist and forced her hand toward the mouth of their zombified pal. Madison squealed and Zoe raced to stop him, but Dustin jumped in front of her, blocking her path. Frankie laughed maniacally, pushing Madison's hand closer and closer. Zack sprinted for Frankie, too, and Dustin spun around, quickly kicking Zack to the ground.

Madison's fingers were inches away from the chomping zombie's incisors. "Uh-ah!" She slipped out of Frankie's grasp, grabbed his arm, and twisted it around his back. She was behind him now, pushing Frankie face-to-face with the zombie prisoner. "You like that?" she taunted him. Frankie put his hand up against the metal grate.

Nom nom nom . . .

"Ow! It bit me!" Frankie clutched his hand between his knees and yowled.

Off the thug's radar, Zack crawled quickly on the

floor and crouched down on all fours behind Dustin's legs. Zoe saw her brother and charged Dustin, who tripped over Zack and fell backward on his tailbone.

"Run!" Zack, Zoe, Madison, and Twinkles raced away from the mallrats.

Vrrrrrrooooom! Rice and Ozzie sped around the corner on their Segways.

"Hey!" Dustin scrambled to his feet. "Get back here!"

Zack and Madison hopped on the Segways piggyback-style and rode off—Zack on Rice's, Madison on Ozzie's. Zoe raced over to a kiosk in the middle of the floor and picked up the mountain bike that Rice and Ozzie had planted there.

"Stop them at the elevators!" Dustin shouted.

"He bit me!" Frankie kicked the cookie stand, rattling the gate.

"Well, they have the antidote, stupid!" Dustin grabbed his skateboard and took off down a nearby escalator. Frankie hopped in the golf cart and zipped through the gargantuan mall, speeding after them.

Zoe pedaled standing up on the bike, gaining speed, but Frankie caught up to her quickly in the motorized cart. They were neck and neck. Frankie jerked the wheel, trying to sideswipe Zoe over the railing.

Zoe swerved to the left. "Chill out, psycho!"

Up ahead, Zack and Rice scooted inside the elevator along with Madison, Ozzie, Twinkles, and the shopping cart arsenal.

"Ditch the bike, Zo!" Madison yelled.

Racing ahead of Frankie, Zoe squeezed the handlebars, leaped off the bicycle, and sprinted into the elevator. Zack punched the DOOR CLOSE button.

Frankie slammed on the gas, bulldozing the discarded bicycle forward with the nose of the golf cart.

"Come on," Zack whined as the big bully plowed toward them. "Close already!"

The elevator doors shut, and a monstrous crash resounded as Frankie slammed into the stainless steel doors. *Ding!* The elevator reopened.

Frankie sauntered into the doorframe. "Now you're all in big, big trouble." He yanked the bike out of the elevator and tossed it behind him. "Who's first?" The too-tall manling eenie-meenied with his index finger.

"Eww," Madison pointed to the bitemark on Frankie's fingertip. "You're bleeding."

"Give me the medicine, you little twerp!" Frankie moved aggressively for Zack. "The real one." Twinkles growled, flashing his puppy fangs. Before Frankie could take another step, the little dog leaped out of Madison's arms, bounded off the ground, and latched onto the fly of the bully's jeans. Frankie let out a girlish squeal, trying to swat the dog away. He dropped to his knees and looked up in desperation, now face-to-face with Zack, who had just finished pulling on a bright red boxing glove from the shopping cart.

Zack wound up and popped the bully in the nose, sending the big goon swooning back into the hall and stumbling to the floor. Frankie's infected hand bulged with gray-green veins, shooting ominously up his arm.

The doors closed, and Zoe nudged Zack. "Nice shot, little bro!"

"Couldn't have done it without Twinkles," Zack said, scratching the Boggle pup behind the ear. "That was a low blow, little guy."

The elevator descended and opened on the second floor. *I pressed* ONE, Zack thought. *What the heck is going on?*

"*Blargh!*" The zombie mall cops staggered toward them, triggering the automatic sensor in the elevator doors. *Ding!* Rice gripped the push-bar on the shopping cart and drove the mall cops back into the hallway.

Ozzie shot out of the elevator on his Segway and stopped between the two undead security guards. They lurched forward to grab the Segway, but Ozzie started to spin in a tight, fast circle like a figure skater at the end of a routine. He kicked his cast up high, blasting the zombies on their chins with a cyclone of roundhouses. Ozzie slowed to a standstill while the zombies swayed in the ripple of his matrix before collapsing to the floor in a slimy heap.

Zack, Rice, Zoe, and Madison watched in awe of their friend's unstoppable martial artistry. Ozzie bowed and scooted back in the elevator with the rest of them.

Just then, on the other side of the mall, Zack spotted Dustin unlocking a store packed with zombies.

"Release the Kraken!" Dustin shouted, throwing up the gate with a flourish. The ravenous consumers swarmed from the department store, zombifying the entire second floor.

"Dustin's lost his mind!" Zack hit the first-floor button one more time and they plummeted downward.

When the doors opened again, the whole level was still teeming with zombie maniacs—store employees, shoppers, moviegoers, and mallrats. Hopelessly out-numbered, only one option remained.

"Zack, hit the button! Hit the button! Hit it!" Rice ordered him, as the zombies all turned their heads at once toward the elevator.

Zack hit the LL button, and they dropped down to the lower level. The doors opened this time to a rush of water, rising fast up to their waists. "Uck!" Madison yelled. "What the heck?"

"Great." Zoe hiked up her dress. "This thing is dry-clean only."

Down the hallway a big sign flickered: UNDERWATER ADVENTURES.

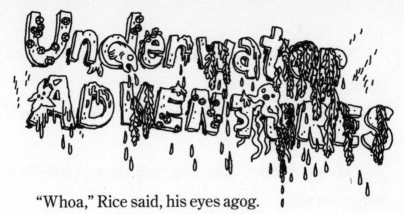

Underwater Adventures

"Whoa," Rice said, his eyes agog. "I didn't know they had an aquarium!"

"Come on," Ozzie said. "There's got to be an exit out of this place."

"What about all our stuff?" Zack pointed to the shopping cart full of gear.

"We'll take what we can." Ozzie opened up two duffel bags, and they stuffed them full of bats and rackets, helmets and pads. Zack and Rice shouldered the bags while Ozzie forged ahead on his crutches between Madison and Zoe as they waded through the dark, dank passageway.

Halfway down, Rice stopped and stared at the informational plaque on the wall next to a busted aquarium window.

"Rice, what are you doing?" asked Zack.

A look of fear came across Rice's face. "Nobody move."

"Why?" asked Madison, pausing mid-step like a game of freeze tag.

"We got sharks," Rice informed them in a deliberately calm voice.

Just then the water swished nearby.

"OMG, I saw a fin!" Madison squealed.

"Everybody, be cool," Rice said. "We just gotta move slow. Sharks are attracted to quick movements." Something underwater nudged the back of Zack's calf muscle. He shuddered and kept on.

"Duh-nuh . . . duh-nuh." Rice hummed the theme song from *Jaws*.

"Dude, please," Zack said. "Not now."

"Sorry."

"*Blahhh!*" A zombie freak shot up out of the water, covered in seaweed.

"Ahhh!" Zoe screamed as the undead lagoon monster dove at them, making a huge splash. Zoe raised a baseball bat over her head, waiting for the splish-splashing ghoul to shoot up again.

"*Rahhhhh!*" The goon resurfaced. Zoe quickly conked the pruny-skinned beast on the noggin, and it slumped down in the waist-deep zombie lagoon.

"Where's Twinkles?" Madison asked, sloshing toward the EMERGENCY EXIT sign at the end of the hall.

"Arf!" The little puppy doggy-paddled behind her. Madison snatched Twinkles up out of the water. "Arf!" Twinkles chirruped.

"Shhhh!" Rice pressed his finger to his lips. "Tell that little piece of shark bait to shut his yapper!"

They moved into a tunnel that had a round glass ceiling, revealing the shark exhibit. It looked like they were walking on the ocean floor. A zombified shark with rows of razor-sharp teeth bashed its snout into the glass, and the whole ceiling shook.

"Let's blow this joint," Rice said, looking up at the mighty predator. "I don't want to mess with any zombie sharks . . . no matter how awesome they are."

As Rice, Ozzie, Zack, Madison, and Twinkles reached the door, the water churned under the surface. Suddenly, Zoe screamed as an unseen force pulled her under. She came up gasping, soaking wet, and clutching her head. Zoe shrieked. A zombie had her by the hair.

"I'm coming, Zo!" Madison yelled and shoved

Twinkles into Rice's arms. She dove into the waist-deep water as a big shark fin glided toward the melee. Right before Madison reached Zoe, the shark's head erupted out of the water with its mouth open wide.

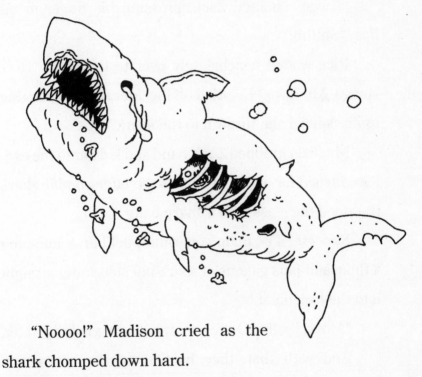

"Noooo!" Madison cried as the shark chomped down hard.

Black blood spurted everywhere, and Zoe let out an ear-piercing scream. "Eeeeee!"

The shark writhed in the shallow water, devouring the zombie hair-puller whose chomputated forearm was still gripping Zoe's hair.

"Eeeeeeeeeeek!" Madison and Zoe shrieked simultaneously.

CRACK! The aquarium glass above them began to splinter.

"Guys!" shouted Zack, pressing his finger to his lips. "Shhhh!"

Rice waded nonchalantly over to the girls. "Here you go, Mr. Jaws." He pried off the undead hand clinging to Zoe's head and threw it to the shark.

Madison grabbed Zoe's hand and led her to the exit. Rice turned for one final look as the huge zombie shark thumped the glass with a sharp bang.

Swooosh! The main aquarium pool burst, dumping a thousand-plus gallons of shark-infested water straight into the basement.

"Move!" yelled Ozzie over the roar of gushing water.

And with that, they hustled up the emergency staircase, the water level rising rapidly behind them.

CHAPTER

O zzie burst through the door, and the seawater gushed out from the overflowing basement.

Rice hopped to his feet and set Twinkles down. "That was insane!"

Zack's eyes bugged out. "What took you guys so long back there?"

Rice tapped his forehead and reached into the front pocket of his pack. He pulled out a brand new iPhone and clutched it to his breast. "It's dry!"

Zack shook his head. He should have guessed.

Zoe shook off the sea plants from her arms, while Madison tapped the water from her ears. "I'm never going to the mall again."

That'll be the day, Zack thought. His adrenaline pumped steadily as he raced around the outside of the mall to where they parked the Winnebago.

Just as the gang filed into the vehicle, Zack looked back toward the mall entrance. The doors shot open, and out ran Dustin with a zombie swarm pouring behind him. The mean boy grappled with a zombified soccer mom grabbing him by the arm. Dustin spun and flung

the undead woman to the concrete. Then he glanced up and locked eyes with Zack.

"Go, go, go!" Zack yelled, as Dustin broke into a sprint for the RV.

Ozzie revved the engine. Zack jumped onboard, and they sped away from the curb. Zack darted to the back and peered out the window, but Dustin was gone.

"What's the matter, Zack?" Rice asked.

Thud-thump-thunk.

"He's up there!" Zack eyed the ceiling of the RV.

"Who?" asked Ozzie.

"Dustin," Zack told him. Ozzie slowed down and pulled over on a deserted side street. "What are you doing?" he asked.

"He doesn't have his muscle anymore," Ozzie said. "Come on."

They all hopped out of the Winnebago together and stared up at Dustin crouched on the roof of the Winnebago. Ozzie pointed at him with his crutch. "Get down, chump!"

"Why don't you make me?"

"We will, stupid," Madison said. "There're five of us and only one of you." Twinkles arfed. "Make that six."

Dustin climbed down hesitantly without taking his eyes off them. His hair stuck straight in the air, and his clothes were all torn up. "Where's Frankie?"

"He's a zombie now . . . ," Zack said.

Zoe chimed in. "Because you had to be a jerk and dognap our puppy."

"Have a nice life, loser." Madison pulled her hair

back in a ponytail and stuck out her tongue. "Let's get out of here."

"Wait, wait, let me come with you . . ." Dustin's voice was almost pathetic.

"We can't trust you, man," Zack said. "Get real."

"I'll be good, I promise." Dustin fell to his knees and clasped his hands.

"I have an idea," Zoe said. "Why don't we let Twinkles decide."

"Whaddaya say?" Dustin crawled on hands and knees to the little pup. "Wanna let me off the hook just for old time's sake?"

Twinkles showed his teeth and growled viciously. The verdict was in.

Dustin snorted in disbelief. "So, what, you'll just leave me here alone to die?"

"Looks like you're doing a pretty good job of that already." Rice pointed to the back of Dustin's arm. "Undying, that is."

"Huh?" Dustin lifted his elbow and peeked under his arm. A zombie tooth was lodged in his skin like a splinter. "Ahhh! What the—" He grimaced and plucked the rotting bicuspid from his arm, then looked up. "Wait!" he said. "You've got the antidote."

"I don't know," Zoe said. "Seems wasteful."

"Just one dose. Come on, I'm begging you." Dustin was on the ground again, kissing Zack's new waterlogged sneakers.

"Just give him a dose and let's get out of here." Zack pulled his foot away. "I'm sick of lookin' at him."

"Okay, stupid," Madison ordered Dustin. "Put your hands behind your back and open your mouth."

Rice unzipped his backpack and dug around in the pocket. "Ummm . . ." He looked up from the bag, and a stark frown fell over his face.

"What's the matter?" Zack asked.

Rice pulled the antidote vial out of the bag. A tiny splash of red serum was all that remained. "There's still a little bit left." Rice said sheepishly, trying to look on the bright side.

A sick panic rose in Zack's chest, as he stared at the empty vial. "What the? How did it?" he stammered.

"The cap must have come loose or something . . . ," Rice guessed.

"Well, you heard him," Dustin said. "There's still a little left. Lemme just—*Blaaaarrrgh!*" Red viral streaks climbed up his neck, and his skin turned a deep shade of green. The zombifying bully dropped to his knees, frothing at the mouth, then fell limp on the pavement.

Rice stepped forward. "You all right, dude?"

Dustin's neck snapped around. His blank eyes opened and bulged with pure undead evil. "Guess not . . ." Rice chuckled nervously and edged away from the zombie punk.

"*Rarrrgh!*" Zombie Dustin sprang off the ground and lunged at them like a rabid dog.

Zoe sprang into action and grabbed Dustin by the wrist. In one swift movement, she twisted his arm behind his back and swept his legs out, putting the undead bully flat on the ground. "There! Let's get out of here!" she said, taking off for the RV.

"He reminded me of Greg a little bit," Rice said, buckling his seatbelt, safe inside. "All cowering on the roof."

"Those guys were worse than Bansal-Jones any day of the week," said Zoe.

"I wonder what Greg's doing right now," Madison said. "Do you think he's still at the army base?"

"He's probably still sucking his thumb," said Ozzie, laughing.

"Okay, guys." Zack went serious. "No more stops until Montana. Deal?"

"Deal!"

 CHAPTER 15

It was after midnight, and almost everyone was asleep. Madison had taken over driving detail and Zack sat, anxiously petting Twinkles on his lap.

"You okay?" She yawned.

Zack gave her a shrug like "Whatever" and stared out the window. They sailed across the Dakota wastelands into Montana, and his eyes glazed over like a zombie's as he rested his chin in the palm of his hand. He didn't know what to think. There were too many ifs. The facts seemed jumbled, and now with a mere drop of the only known cure that remained—what if it wasn't enough? And what if Madison couldn't produce any-more? He didn't want to think about that, though. Not right now, anyway.

"It'll be okay, Zack," Madison said, as if reading his mind. "I'm worried, too."

"You are?" Zack looked at the semi-reformed mean girl. Zack shrugged. "You just never seem like you worry about anything."

"I mean, like, I have no idea where my parents are right now."

"Maybe they made it to Tucson?" Zack said, not wanting to upset her.

"What's the difference?" Madison mumbled blankly. "They're probably zombies, too."

"What'd they do to you in Washington, anyway?" Zack changed the subject.

"You thought zombies were bad?" said Madison. "Those scientist guys were, like, worse than vampires."

"That's pretty messed up," Zack said solemnly.

Madison gazed off down the highway. "They did the same thing in Tucson," she said. "Took a bunch of samples for themselves and then put me on the helicopter for the next guy. Now I can't help anyone."

"So wait," Zack interrupted. "Tucson has some of the antidote?"

"I guess, unless they used it up already—" Madison shrieked and jerked the wheel. The RV fishtailed and nearly tipped as they screeched to a halt in the middle of the road.

"Madison, what are you doing?" Zack steadied his hand on the dashboard.

"Did you see that?" She gasped.

"See what?"

"I think it was a zombie . . . or a deer, maybe." Madison yawned again, then tensed up, her eyes shooting from side to side. "What was that?"

"What was what?"

"You didn't hear that?" She gulped.

Zack listened for the noise he hadn't heard. A hand slapped down on his shoulder, and Zack whipped his head around.

Ozzie squinted at him with bleary eyes, half awake. "I think we're all a little pooped, Zack. Maybe we ought to pack it in for the night."

"That's probably a good idea," Zack agreed.

"It's a good place to stop, anyway," Ozzie said, looking out at the desolate plain surrounding them. "No zombies all the way out here . . ."

They pulled over on the barren stretch of road to hunker down for the night. As she put the Winnebago into park, Madison glared at the boys. "I'm not crazy, you know. I did see something."

Sure you did, Zack thought. He gazed out the passenger window at the uninhabited wasteland and then closed his eyes.

Zack woke up in the passenger seat, blinded by the sunlight piercing the windshield. He hobbled stiffly out of the front seat, squinting at the day.

Rice and Ozzie were doing warm-ups outside, stretching and practicing their martial arts moves. Zoe and Madison were making a batch of microwave popcorn in the back of the Winnebago.

"Good morning, Zacky-poo," said Zoe. "Care for some of Orville's finest butter-free popcorn?"

"It's the only kind I can eat," Madison said. "I mean, veganly speaking."

"Where are the Ho-Hos?" Zack wiped a little crustball of sleep from his eye.

"All gone," Zoe said.

"What are you talking about?" said Zack. "We had four boxes."

"Talk to your boy," Madison said.

Rice and Ozzie came through the door into the back of the

Winnebago, glossy with sweat from their morning workout.

"Ugh," Rice said, clutching at a cramp in his side. "Being a ninja is hard."

"It's a lot of work," Ozzie said, relaxing on the floor with his cast elevated on one of the seats. "But you'll get there, Rice. You've got the love."

"Is it as hard as eating four boxes of Ho-Hos?" Zack challenged him.

"I only ate two." Rice defended himself. "Zoe ate the rest."

Zack glared at his sister.

Zoe shrugged her shoulders. "I was hungry."

"Whatever," Zack said. "You guys ready to hit the road?"

"Ready like Freddy."

"Just let me know when we get to Duplessis," Zoe said, pulling a sleep mask down over her eyes. "I need my beauty rest."

"Yeah, you do." Rice snickered.

Zoe belted him in the head with a pillow.

Ozzie started the engine. "Which way am I going?" he asked.

"Hold on." Rice Google-mapped the BurgerDog ranch on his new iPhone and then pointed down the westbound highway.

Ozzie pulled back onto the interstate, and a cloud of dirt swirled up from the tires as the Winnebago shot into the badlands of Montana.

CHAPTER 16

They drove for hours toward the rugged chain of mountains in the distance before finally spotting an access road on the outskirts of the BurgerDog cattle ranch. "You guys, I think this is it," Rice said, looking at his smartphone.

They hung a right and found themselves driving through an endless grid of cooped-up cattle. Behind the industrial fencing, cows roamed everywhere, mooing and cawing. But as they moved deeper into the ranchland, Zack got a closer look at Duplessis's bovine hogs.

The genetically engineered animals had big pig noses with horned cow heads, fat pig bodies with cow fur, and long curly cow tails. The mutated beasts snuffled and stamped the dirt with their hooves. Some of them had two snouts sprouting out of the same head with one Cyclops eye between them.

"Ew, little bro." Zoe gagged. "You ate one of those things."

"I have a feeling I'm not going to like this place," said Madison.

Beyond the front gates of BurgerDog headquarters, a swarm of zombie people mingled with undead livestock.

Ozzie guided the Winnebago down a side road that curved around the main complex. He slowed to a stop beside a large square blue warehouse.

"Put your game faces on." Ozzie shut off the engine and hopped out.

They geared up, donning helmets and pads and arming themselves with bludgeons and bats. At the rear entrance next to the loading docks, a keycard scanner glowed with a tiny red dot next to the locked door. "Wait here," Zack said and ran toward the fence,

where a BurgerDog factory worker clung with both hands on the other side of the chain-link.

"Thank you . . . Mr. Pendleton," Zack said, plucking off the ID tag clipped to the foreman's breast pocket.

"Zack, look out!" Rice yelled to his buddy.

Zack glanced around the zombie's girth and saw a genetically mutated bovine hog charging straight for him. Zack jumped back as the undead livestock rammed into Mr. Pendleton and then toppled the fence posts. Zack took off for the access door as the foreman and the cow-pig lumbered toward him over the fallen chain-link fence.

Zack swiped the keycard and the red dot blipped green.

"Here we go." Zoe plugged her nose and stepped across the threshold.

The emergency lights flickered and snapped as the whole gang lurked through the dimly lit corridor. Straight ahead, a Siamese zombie cow-pig conjoined at the skull with two separate bodies—one all pig, one completely cow—scrabbled toward them on eight legs like a giant mammalian spider. The half-hog-half-heifer's heads were fused together into one horrific honking mutant cattle.

"Okey-dokey," Madison said queasily. "Other way!"

They scurried down another cement-reinforced hallway, pushing deeper and deeper into the compound. A dense mass of zombies ticked spasmodically toward them. Cattle ranchers in Stetsons, BurgerDog meat packers in white hard hats, factory workers wearing hairnets and dust masks stumbled mindlessly in different directions, raking the air with their lethal claws.

Zack screeched to a stop as the zombies cast their reptilian eyes upon them, gargling on juicy intakes of slime.

"Over here!" Ozzie shouted, and they ran through a series of identical corridors until they came to a door labeled TESTING LEVEL D.

They pushed through the swinging doors and found themselves standing on a high narrow deck, ten feet above the floor of a huge room. Below them, conveyer belts ran on zigzags like moving sidewalks. Yellow-and-black-striped caution levers jutted out of the smooth, high cement walls. Forklifts with pallets stacked with boxes upon boxes of unrefrigerated beef patties lay spilled on the floor.

Behind them, the automatic doors parted, and zombie food scientists, cattle ranchers, and meat packers stumbled inside, tumbling onto the platform.

The gang raced around the catwalk, down a ladder, and onto a lower level. Ahead, a set of stairs leading to the plant floor was covered in pork-beef slime. The BurgerDog patties were twitching and squirming off the conveyer belts worming along the floor.

The legion of undead factory employees and cattle ranchers began to topple down the staircase like a waterfall of walking corpses, spilling undead-over-heels to the production level.

"Go!" Zack shouted. Ozzie led the way, swinging on his crutches to the ground floor.

Under the conveyor belts, the scraps of raw meat quivered and jiggled, clumping together and inching toward a common point. In the center of the room, a massive blob of rotting meat-flesh pulsated on the ground like a cocoon.

They all stopped dead in their tracks. Zoe covered her mouth and nose, ready to hurl. Twinkles sniffed the bulging ball of meat and made a sour face. Zack looked back at the zombies closing in behind them.

The beefy blob started to grow, sculpting itself up into an eight-foot-tall tongue-shaped glob. The hunk of BurgerDog chuck then sprouted crude appendages made entirely of the mange-mottled meat. Rice stared silently, in awe of the humongous zombie meatball.

"I'm just gonna go out on a limb here and say that's the nastiest freakin' thing I've ever seen in my life," Ozzie said as the green maggoty meat monster stomped toward them, one foot forward like a Claymation Beefzilla.

"Let's get the heck out of here!" Zack yelled, taking off for the other side of the room. A yellow forklift blocked the emergency exit door.

The zombified BurgerDog employees staggered across the room, flanking the meat behemoth.

"Owwwwww!" Rice howled. "Something bit me!"

"Nothing bit you!" Zack shouted, losing his patience.

"I'm serious this time," said the boy who cried zombie. Rice bent over and lifted his pantleg. "Gah!" A piece of BurgerDog meat in the shape of a slug sucked at his skin like a leech. Rice plucked the thing off with a pop.

"Ew, Rice!" Madison cringed and covered her eyes. Zack watched as a thick runnel of black blood streamed down Rice's calf.

He wasn't faking.

"Whoa!" Ozzie yelled, and pointed behind him at the zombie meat man. Three long phalanges of beef branched out of the arms. The toxic meat monster swung its new hands through the air, probing with its tentacles.

"Rice, let's get out of—" Zack started to say when an ugly spasm crossed his buddy's face.

"Dude," Rice looked him dead in the eyes, whispering

feebly. "Turning into a zombie is way less cool than I thought it would be . . ." Rice's eyes rolled back, and he started to keel over.

"Hey!" Zack caught his undying buddy and dropped to one knee. Rice slumped over Zack's leg.

He was dead weight.

"**C**ome on, Zack!" Zoe screamed. "We had to get the heck out of here, like, five minutes ago!"

"The meat dude's gonna eat us!" Madison yelled. "This is so not how I'm supposed to die."

The BurgerDog meat man stomped forward, its huge beefy feet squelching with every stride. The zombified workforce raged around the boneless meat monster towering above them. The inhuman moan was a deafening, deep-throated bellowing.

Zack unslung Rice's arms from the shoulder straps of his backpack and propped him up to a seated position.

"You're not giving him the antidote!" Zoe said.

"I'm not," Zack said. "But we can't leave him. Gimme a hand."

Zoe and Madison helped Zack lug Rice through the door, while Ozzie hopped into the seat of a forklift and turned on the motor.

The great Globzilla took a long step toward the exit and catapulted its meaty arm at the door.

Ozzie lined the vehicle up and raised the forklift as high as it would go. He hit the gas pedal and zoomed into the meat giant full force. Zack watched from the doorway as Ozzie rammed the forklift into the wall, splattering the mammoth meat man to pieces.

"Ozzie!" Zack shouted, holding the door for his friend. "Hurry up!" With the zombies surging behind him, Ozzie hop-stepped through the exit on his crutches, and the door slammed behind them.

Outside in the hall, a nasty rash spread quickly up Rice's neck. He began to look pale, then white, and finally yellow.

"Give him some ginkgo!" Ozzie suggested.

"Not yet," Zack said. "We don't want to have to drag him."

Rice's zombified eyes popped open, and Zack quickly snapped the chinstrap on his buddy's helmet, pulling it tight and secure over his snarling face.

Zack led Rice by their old dog leash as they slowly made their way through the labyrinth of hallways. In front of them, an undead cattle rancher lurched around the corner. "*Blargh!*" Ozzie poked his crutch at the ground like a garbage picker, threading it through the gap between the zombie's legs. The six-foot-six brawny beast tripped to the floor with a bone-crunching *splat*.

"Come on, Rice!" They urged their buddy on. Rice

snarled and staggered forward a little faster.

They made a quick left and hustled down an empty corridor with an EXIT sign marking the end. Zoe ran ahead and flung open the door. "Hurry! They're coming!" she screamed.

Two separate herds of zombies were converging on their only escape route. Behind them, an undead herd of bovine hogs clomped around the corner.

It was all or nothing.

"Come on, Rice!" Zack yanked his zombified friend so hard that Rice fell facemask-first to the floor. Madison grabbed the leash now, too, and she and Zack tug-of-warred backward down the hall as fast as they could.

"*Blaaaahhhh!*" The factory zombies clashed in front of the exit just as Rice's feet dragged across the doorstep. The emergency door slammed shut. Outside the factory,

they all grabbed their knees, gasping for breath.

Zack glanced up and spotted a white clapboard mansion built into the mountain cliff peak. "Up there!" he shouted as the lunatic meat packers busted through the exit.

Twinkles took off ahead, and Zack, Zoe, Madison, Ozzie, and zombie Rice followed, trudging up the one-lane mountain road. Zack dragged Rice along, making sure he didn't wander off the edge. He watched as a beard of slime dribbled from his undead buddy's chin.

Behind them the flesh-eating nincompoops spiraled up the mountain.

At the top, the mansion tapered out from the natural rock of the mountain peak. To the left of the colonial housetop, a long, rectangular second-story window stretched across a wall of stone. It looked like some type of laboratory.

Zack dropped Rice's leash and raced up the steps of the mansion. He pressed the button on the intercom. No answer. "Duplessis, open up!" he called out.

"Hey!" Ozzie pointed up to the laboratory window. Someone was gazing down at them.

"It's the health department," Zack spoke again into the speaker. "We've had some complaints." And just like that, the man ran out of view.

They stood on the stoop of the mansion, watching as the zombies lumbered around the final bend.

"Is he coming?" Zoe asked.

"How am I supposed to know?" Zack shrugged.

Rice grabbed Zoe by the arm and tried to bite her through the facemask. She whapped him hard in the helmet and he let go. "Bad Rice!"

Zack and Ozzie split off in opposite directions, pulling up on all the windows. Madison and Zoe banged on the door, screaming and ringing the doorbell. Rice was moaning and groaning, too, but for different reasons.

The zombie masses were now less than twenty yards away.

"What do we do?" Madison asked.

The undead laborers plodded slowly up the driveway when the peep slot on the door shot open. A pair of eyes peered outside. "Oh dear," said the voice.

"Let us in, mister!" Zack shouted.

The chain jangled and the bolt clacked. The door opened slightly. They all pushed quickly inside past the man and slammed the door.

Thaddeus Duplessis was short and wore a crisp white lab coat. On his head, a thatch of black hair with gray streaks tufted up and out to the sides. It looked like three skunks were sitting on his head with their tails up. Strapped to his forehead were a pair of goggles that made him

look like some kind of four-eyed insect.

"Whoa." Madison bulged her eyes. "Nerd alert."

Duplessis peered out through the peephole at the zombies coming toward the house. "What have you done?" He whipped his head around. "You've set them free!"

"What have *we* done? What have *you* done?" Zoe grabbed the guilty geneticist by the lapel of his lab coat with two fists. "Because of you, I'm going to have a permanent scar right here." She pointed to her forehead. "And here, and here, and here." She shoved the man away, and he knocked back into the wall.

"Yeah, buddy. You've got some serious explaining to do," Ozzie said. "My dad got his arm ripped off because of you."

"And our parents got zombified," Zack said.

"And I don't even know where my family is." Madison cocked her eyebrow.

"And neither does Rice," Zack added. Rice snarled and staggered toward the mad scientist. "Easy, Rice . . ." He pulled his zombified buddy back by the shirt collar.

Professor Duplessis dropped to his knees and burst into sobs. The grown man cried, blubbering, unable to speak.

"Get a hold of yourself, man!" Madison marched up to Duplessis and gave him a firm slap across the cheek.

"Madison!" Ozzie yelled.

"What?" she said. "It always works in old movies."

"Thank you." Duplessis gathered himself, holding the side of his face. "I needed that." He stood up and looked at them. "Come with me."

The BurgerDog creator walked off, and they followed him into the parlor room. A large birdcage hung from the tall ceiling like a chandelier. "It all started after I accomplished the impossible." He glanced up and gestured to the top of the cage, where a pot-bellied pig sat high up on the perch. Duplessis produced a treat from his pocket and made a funny pig sound out of the corner of his mouth. The pig leaped off the bird perch and fluttered down, light as a feather, to the floor of the cage.

"You made a flying pig?" Zack asked.

"Indeed," Duplessis said.

"Why?"

"Because as the saying goes, 'When pigs fly . . .'" A sad smile crossed his face. "Anything is possible. It was a test, and I succeeded."

"I don't care about your stupid Dumbo pig," Zoe told him. "How did the meat turn into zombie burgers?"

"It's very complex." Duplessis sighed. "When we

recombined the DNA from cow to pig, we had to use a strain from a third species to complete the genetic vector. Nothing worked until we used the ectoplasm from a newly discovered deep-sea jellyfish."

Madison scrunched her face. "Dude, you're making, like, zero sense."

I can't believe Rice is missing this, Zack mused as Duplessis continued.

"The life cycle of this particular jellyfish is unlimited due to its magnificent regenerative properties. In other words, it can't die. At first the meat was fine, but then it wasn't . . ." Duplessis sighed. "The rest is history."

"Well, if we don't do something," Zack said, "there won't be any more history."

"Yeah," Madison said. "It'll just be itstory." Twinkles woofed in agreement.

"All I ever wanted was to make some-thing so delicious that no

human being could resist it." Duplessis looked off wistfully. "The burger that tastes like a hotdog."

"Well, why not make something so delicious that no *zombie* could resist it?" Zack suggested.

"It could be done, if only there was a way to reverse the zombification . . ."

"There is," Zack said. "And we've got it." He dug around for the last bit of antidote and pulled out the vial.

"Is this . . . ?" A glimmer of hope flashed in Duplessis's eye.

They all nodded yes.

"Follow me."

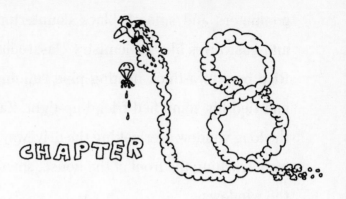

CHAPTER 18

Thaddeus Duplessis led them up a steep staircase and guided them through a maze of corridors. "We're actually inside the mountain," Duplessis told them proudly. "From this tunnel system, I can access almost any part of my facility."

"Big whoop," Zoe said. "You, like, want a prize or something?"

"Is she always this pleasant?" Duplessis asked Zack.

"Always . . ."

Moments later, the geneticist stopped and opened a set of thick steel double doors, which led into a high-tech lab facility. The lab was fully equipped with super-fast computers and smooth black countertops with sinks and gas valves like a chemistry classroom. Zack pulled Rice over to a thick heating pipe running up the wall and tied his zombified friend up tight. Zack stared out the long window overlooking the driveway. The zombies were trashing the front of the house, smashing through the windows.

"Now let me get this straight." Duplessis pointed at Madison. "She's the cure?"

"She was," Zack said. "I mean, she still is . . ."

"She just needs to replenish," Zoe chimed in.

"I see." Duplessis nodded, his mind racing.

"And all we have left is this tiny little bit." Zack handed him the vial.

"We'll have to try and clone the compound."

"You can do that?" Ozzie asked, keeping up on his crutches.

"It may be difficult, but in theory, yes." He ran his hands through his skunk-tail hair. "Then we'll need a way to mass-distribute."

"Huh?" Zack said.

"What do zombies like to eat more than brains?" he mused.

"Nothing, really," Zoe piped in.

"Well, do a little brainstorming then . . . hah!" Duplessis walked over to Rice and studied his zombified face. Rice was fighting against the leash collar, crazy

eyes bulging. Then Duplessis turned to them all. "I'll be back in a flash."

"What a weirdo!" Madison and Zoe jinxed themselves when Duplessis left the room.

"I kind of like him," Ozzie said. "I mean for a guy who zombified everything."

"Come on, guys," Zack said. "Let's think."

"Okay," Zoe started. "Zombies love flesh and brains. I can tell you, because when I was a zombie

those were two very delicious-seeming things."

"So," said Madison. "Whatever it is has to taste like flesh and brains."

"No," Ozzie said. "It has to taste better than flesh and brains."

"But what tastes better than flesh and brains to a zombie?" Zack asked.

"Nothing," Zoe replied, stumped.

Rice growled, chained to the wall. *Man*, Zack thought, *I wish Rice were here. He'd definitely know.*

"Why don't we just use actual brains and marinate them in the antidote first?" Zoe suggested.

"Where are we going to get that many brains, though?" Zack asked her.

"We can put the antidote on pretty much anything." Ozzie thought out loud. "It just has to attract zombies more than we do."

"Like what?"

"How about popcorn?" Madison said. "Everybody likes popcorn."

"Yeah," Zack pondered. "But zombies don't eat popcorn, Madison."

"Fine, whatever. I can't think anymore," Madison moaned. "My brain is fried."

There was a long pause. Zack looked at her out of the corner of his eye.

"That's it!" he exclaimed. "Madison, you're a genius!"

"Well, duh . . . ," she said with a flip of her long, blond ponytail.

Zack began his hypothesis. "You said your brains were fried . . ." He turned to Madison. "What do you like better: chicken fingers or chicken à la king?"

Madison shook her head. "You're asking the wrong girl."

"My bad, I forgot." Zack looked at his sister. "Zoe?"

"Fingers," she said.

"And Ozzie," he continued. "French fries or mashed potatoes?"

"French fries," Ozzie answered. "What's your point?"

"See?" Zack said. "Everything tastes better when it's fried, right? So if we make the zombie junk food taste like fried brains, then . . ."

"But what does fried brain even taste like?"

"You guys are focusing on the wrong stuff," Zack said, exasperated. "We need Duplessis . . . where'd that dude go?"

Just then Duplessis reentered the laboratory. The mad scientist walked silently across the room with his hands clasped behind his back and a solemn expression on his face. Then he spoke: "Which would you like first? The good news or the not-so-good news?"

CHAPTER 19

"Good news first, please," Zoe said biting her thumbnail.

"There was just enough antidote to clone the serum." Duplessis grinned. "We'll have plenty more in just a short while."

"That's great news!" Zack cheered.

"What's the bad news?" Ozzie asked warily.

Duplessis gave them all a wry smile. "There is no bad news. I was just having a little fun. Hah! How did the *brain*storming go?" He chuckled again, quite amused with himself.

Zack smiled. "Can you make something that tastes like fried human brains?"

"In theory, yes. But we'd need a sample of real human brain in order to match the flavor. So, unless one of you is ready to give up your cerebral cortex . . ."

"Wait!" Zack unzipped Rice's backpack and riffled around. Down at the very bottom, he felt the plastic baggie. He pulled out the leftover patty-shaped cross-section of the brain from Mr. Budington's science classroom that they fed to their zombie teachers, all the way back in Phoenix. "How about this?"

Duplessis took the brain sample and strode briskly out of the room, down a long corridor, and into the fast-food testing facility. He brought the brain slice to a stainless steel table with two Fryolators plugged into the wall. He dropped the brain in the sizzling hot oil and let it fry for a minute, then took it out. The vivisected brain looked almost like a BurgerDog patty. Duplessis brought the fried brain over to a fancy machine shaped like a coffeemaker and placed the specimen on a crystal lens, where the hot plate would have been. He hit a switch, and a laser beam scanned back and forth over the patty. "We just need to wait a minute for the bio-sensory readout to process the flavor."

"Oh." Zack nodded his head, pretending to under-stand. "Okay."

Ten minutes later, a sample of the fried brain flavor was ready.

Madison put Twinkles on the table, and Duplessis dropped a small blob of the artificial flavoring into a petri dish. Twinkles looked around nervously and then sniffed the clear, thick, fried-brain-flavored liquid.

"Go on . . ." Madison encouraged the puppy.

Zack waited with rapt anticipation as the tiny dog sniffed it again and then lapped it up.

"How is it, Twinkles?" Madison asked her pup.

"Arf!" The little dog licked his chops and wagged his tail happily.

A short while later, the new batch of antidote and the first round of the fried-brain flavoring were ready.

"What are we going to put it on?" Zack asked.

"Popcorn, Zack," Madison said. "I told you. It even looks like little brains."

"She might be onto something." Duplessis's eyes lit up. "Come with me. I have an idea."

Duplessis walked them through his research center to another warehouselike room. There was a huge metal cylinder with four stainless steel chutes sticking out from the circumference of the round metal vat. The kids stood behind the junk-food geneticist as he operated the controls. Soon, the popcorn started popping in the large industrial kettle and jiggled down the chutes. Another machine spritzed it with the antidote, then finally glazed it with the fried brain flavoring.

While the first batch of the zombie treats finished up, Duplessis ushered them down the steps into the packaging room, where oversize bags of the zombie-corn were already being sealed and toted on the conveyer belts.

"Now, just to be sure, we have to test it on a live specimen," Duplessis said.

"Rice!" Zack grabbed one of the popcorn bags, raced back through the corridors, and burst into the laboratory, where Rice was still tied to the wall.

Zoe, Madison, Ozzie, Twinkles, and Duplessis followed behind Zack as he carefully approached his ravenous pal. Rice looked awful, snarling and gurgling phlegm. Zack took a handful of the unzombification popcorn and sculpted a neat little pile of it on the floor. Once the antidotal snack chow was set, Zack moved a few yards to the side and sat down cross-legged, even with the pile.

"Okay," Zack called. "Unchain him." He crossed his fingers as Duplessis took off Rice's helmet and undid the leash.

Zombie Rice waddled toward his best friend. His eyeballs drooped behind his glasses and his chicken-pox scabs oozed amber slime.

"*Braaaaiins!*" he gurgled, snapping his teeth.

"Zack, watch out!" Zoe screamed. "He's gonna bite you! He doesn't know you're his friend!"

Rice lowered his jaws, ready to snack down on his best bud.

Zack shrank back, tightening his biceps.

As Rice's nose neared Zack, the fried brain smell wafted up, catching his attention. He sniffed the air and grumbled, following the scent to the pile of popcorn on the floor.

"*Braaaaiins!*" he rasped again.

They all watched with excitement as Rice tottered to the popcorn, dropped to his knees, and plunged face-first into the pile, scarfing it up.

Rice chewed the fried-brain-flavored morsels with his mouth open. Flecks of brain-corn flew from his pie-hole as he nibbled his undead fingertips and licked his clammy palms.

"So grody." Madison cringed.

Zombie Rice glanced around with a crazed look on his face, breathing loudly through his mouth before collapsing on the floor.

"Rice!" Zack crouched down and shook his buddy.

Rice's eyes popped open, and he smiled groggily. "Gotcha..."

"You're right, Rice." Zack's eyes lit with laughter as he helped his best friend to his feet. "You really did."

"Ew, Rice." Zoe plugged her nose. "You're, like, all smelly."

"Dude, I was a zombie!" Rice smiled and popped his collar. The slimy pock marks on his face were already drying up.

"Welcome back, ninja warrior," Ozzie said, bowing

with respect. "We gotta get going though."

With Rice in tow, they went back to the snack manufacturing division and carried the big industrial-size bags of popcorn up to the laboratory.

From the window, Zack could see an endless horde of zombies thronging into Duplessis's estate.

"This way." Duplessis marched through the second floor to the balcony overlooking the entrance hall of his home. The senseless maniacs pillaged through the foyer, thrashing the furniture and tearing down the pictures from the walls. Duplessis's winged piglet flapped and fluttered wildly, oinking in the birdcage.

Zack ripped open a bag of brain bites and launched the kernels of antidote, showering the ransacking zombies now stomping up the twin spiral staircases to the landing.

But the zombies didn't go for the popcorn.

"Oh no!" Madison cried. "It's not working!"

"But it worked on Rice . . ."

"That's because he's Rice," Zoe said. "He'll eat anything!"

Rice shrugged. "She's probably right."

"Look!" Duplessis pointed as the zombies began to zero in on the popcorn treats. The undead maniacs dropped to the ground and gobbled up the popcorn with their disgusting, boil-covered tongues.

As the zombies

guzzled the popcorn, the horde began to collapse, one by one.

Zack, Rice, Ozzie, Madison, Zoe, Twinkles, and Duplessis hustled downstairs through the unzombifying swarm to the front entrance of the estate. On the front porch, they flung open bags of popcorn over the rest of the zombie crowd until the last of the flesh-eating savages passed out.

They gazed out at the great heap of twisted limbs and distended skulls and watched in utter silence as the cattle ranchers, meat packers, and food scientists regained their humanity.

The repentant geneticist stared at his re-reanimated zombloyees, and a tear ran down his cheek. He looked at Zack and the rest of them graciously. "Thank you," he said softly. "Thank you . . ."

"You're welcome," Zack said. "But you have to cross your heart and hope to die that you'll never genetically engineer another animal for the rest of your life."

Duplessis made an *X* over his breast pocket and mumbled something quietly to himself. "I promise," he said.

"And you have to apologize," Madison said.

"I'm sorry." Duplessis frowned.

"Not to us," she said. "To them." Madison pointed to the crowd of unzombified people standing bewildered in the driveway.

Duplessis faced his former staff and projected his voice. "Sorry, everyone!"

The people grumbled, rubbing their faces and staring at their surroundings. They still looked confused. "My thumb!" a grown man yelped. "It's gone!"

Duplessis turned back to the kids. "I'll give them some time to recover."

"You're in charge again," Zack said, patting Duplessis on the back. "Don't screw it up." He slung a popcorn bag over his shoulder and walked down the stairs. "Come on, guys," Zack said to the rest of the gang.

The befuddled mass of formerly undead BurgerDog employees parted, allowing a path for the five heroic kids and their little dog, too.

The sunset sky flamed red and orange as the Winnebago rolled up the mountain road. Zack sat in the front, while Ozzie drove. Rice stuck his head in between the seats. "You guys need to fill me in on what happened, you know."

"We will, Rice," Zack said. "Don't worry."

Behind the Winnebago, Zoe steered a giant eighteen-wheeler delivery truck up the narrow, spiraling road. Madison was petting Twinkles in the passenger seat. *Honk-honk!* Zoe pulled the cord to blow the truck's horn.

When they pulled back up to the mansion, Duplessis was waiting with hundreds of popcorn bags ready to go. The whole gang hopped out and loaded them into the back of their rides.

"Where will you go now?" Duplessis asked Zack as they prepared to leave.

"Phoenix, Arizona." Zack handed him a little pad of paper from Rice's backpack. "Write down your number. We'll need more of this eventually."

Duplessis scribbled down his contact info and looked up. "What are you going to do in Phoenix?"

"We're gonna get our families back."

CHAPTER

The stars shone brightly in the pitch-dark sky as they approached Phoenix with a massive delivery of unzombifying popcorn. In front of them, Twinkles hung his head out the passenger window of the eighteen-wheeler.

"Tuesday night." Zack sighed to himself.

This time last week, he'd been in bed, lights out, trying to will himself to sleep. Zoe was in her room doing Zoe things. Mom and Dad were downstairs doing Mom-and-Dad things. He couldn't wait to return his parents to their normal form. He liked normal. Normal was good.

Next to him Ozzie stared out the windshield with a blank look on his face.

Zack looked over from the passenger seat. "You okay, man?"

"Huh?" Ozzie shook the daydream out of his head. "I was just thinkin', everything isn't just going to be fine now that we have all this popcorn or whatever . . ."

"It isn't . . . ?" Zack asked. "Why not?"

"No, I mean, like, my dad," Ozzie continued. "Just because we unzombify him doesn't mean he's gonna grow another arm, you know?"

"That's true . . . ," Zack said, trailing off. He hadn't even thought about that. He was so glad that his zombified parents were safe, locked inside the bank vault with all of their body parts intact.

"Don't worry, Oz," Rice said from the backseat. "Once we find my dad, he can give your dad a new arm."

"How's he gonna do that?" Ozzie scoffed.

"He's a prosthetic surgeon," Rice said, chewing something with his mouth full.

"Rice, what are you eating?" Zack asked.

"These things are actually pretty tasty," Rice said, popping a fistful of the zombie popcorn into his mouth.

"Dude, quit eating those." Zack scolded his pal. "It's for the zombies."

Just then, Zoe's voice crackled over the radio static. "Hey, little bro," she said. "Looks like we've got some company up ahead."

Ozzie had rigged one of the security guard radios to the dashboard and tuned into the same broadband frequency as the one Zoe and Madison kept on the truck's two-way.

A military roadblock obstructed the interstate in front of them, and they slowed down. Two soldiers walked toward them with their palms out. One of them marched to the semi, and Zoe poked her head through the open driver's-side window. The other one approached the boys in the Winnebago. The big broad-shouldered soldier peered inside. "Ozzie?"

Zack thought he looked familiar. If it wasn't for the three-day beard, he would have looked just like . . .

"*Sergeant Patrick?*" Ozzie asked.

"Ozzie Briggs," Sgt. Patrick said with a wide smile. "The colonel's gonna be mighty glad to see you."

"My dad's a zombie . . ."

"Yeah," Rice said to the Sergeant. "And you're supposed to be a zombie, too."

"Not me," Patrick replied, gazing off to retell the tale. "After the base went into lockdown, I was trapped outside, dodging zombies left and right. I looked up to the control room, the only room that can undo

emergency shutdown, and then I see that idiot kid in the soccer uniform you were with—"

"NotGreg?" Rice suggested, listening with rapt attention.

"Yeah, Greg," Sergeant Patrick continued. "I told him to duck down so I could fire my gun, break the glass, and tell him how to disengage the lockdown protocol. He did everything I said, mostly right. Then I raced back to the medic unit where they kept the blood samples from that Madalyn girl."

"Madison," said Zack.

"Who cares," said Rice. "What happened next?"

"Well, Greg and I unzombified Private Michaels, and from there we made it to the hangar where the rest of the survivors were quarantined. After rounding up all the humans, we decided to head northbound to Phoenix. But just after we hit the road, this one-armed zombie staggered in front of my Jeep."

"My dad!" Ozzie's voice rose with excitement.

"Yep, Colonel Briggs. So I pulled over and gave him the last sample I had. That was four days ago."

"Is he here?" Ozzie asked.

Sergeant Patrick pointed up the road. "Take that first exit into downtown. There's a command post a few blocks in. You can't miss it."

"Thank you, sir." Zack tossed him a bag of the unzombifying popcorn.

"What's this?" The Sergeant's eyes widened at the bag. "I love caramel corn!"

"Zombie-corn." Zack smiled. "Not for eating . . . for feeding."

They led the eighteen-wheeler into downtown Phoenix and stopped at a military-style base camp in the center of their hometown. Rows of camouflaged tents lined the outside of the county hospital.

Inside one of the tents, tables were set up with radio equipment and portable electronics gear. A large man with one arm leaned on one of the tables with his back to them, speaking into a radio receiver.

"What do you mean, they're all coming? Well, stop them, that's what you're there for!" The man paused. "What do you mean there's too many?"

"Dad!" Ozzie shouted and ran to the colonel, throwing his arms around his father's waist. The colonel stood up and looked down, startled by the appearance of his only son.

"I'll call you back . . ." The colonel dropped the phone, picked Ozzie up with one arm, and spun him around. "What happened to your leg?" he said, setting Ozzie down.

"I broke it," Ozzie said. "But I'm okay."

All of a sudden, a surprisingly young-looking soldier marched over to the colonel. "Sir, we're receiving reports all around the city, all saying the same thing: The zombies are doubling back on us, sir!"

Colonel Briggs scratched his head, nostrils flaring. "It doesn't make sense."

Zack studied the smallish soldier for a moment and then crinkled his eyebrows. "Greg?" he said, nudging his sister. Zoe and Madison gazed at Greg Bansal-Jones with amazement.

"Hey, Greg," Madison said.

Greg looked at Zoe, Zack, Madison, and Rice

blankly. "I'm sorry, have we met?"

"Uh, yeah?" Zoe said. "We have, like, all the same classes together, dummy."

"I'm sorry, miss," Greg said. "But I have no idea what you're talking about."

"I'm confused," Rice said. "Is he NotGreg still, or Greg again?"

In a matter of days, Greg Bansal-Jones had transformed from a world-class middle school bully into a hideous zombie freak, then into an unzombified dummy with amnesia who only responded to NotGreg. The amnesia remained, but now it seemed NotGreg was a dedicated, obedient soldier.

"I don't know," Zack said. "I'm as confused as you are."

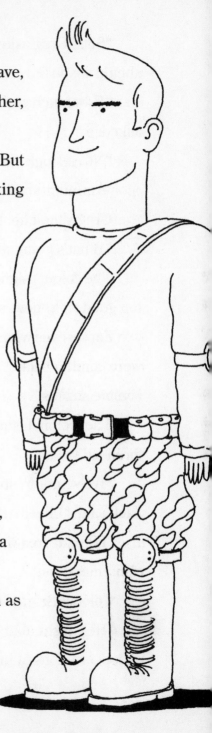

"Sir?" Greg asked for the colonel's attention. "What should we do?"

"How much ginkgo do we have left?" Colonel Briggs asked.

"Not enough, sir," Greg said.

"Ammunition?"

Greg shook his head. "Uh-uh."

"What's going on, Dad?" Ozzie asked.

The colonel sighed a hopeless sigh. "It's not looking too good right now, son."

Zack's eyes widened as he realized why the zombies were coming back. "The truck," he said. "It's filled with zombie snacks!"

The colonel squinted at Zack and furrowed his forehead.

"We've got to spread the popcorn around the city," Zack said. "Like in a big circle."

"Like a freakin' forcefield!" Rice erupted with excitement.

Colonel Briggs looked skeptical.

"He's right, dad," Ozzie said. "We have a truck full of popcorn doused in the antidote."

"Well, why didn't you say so?" The colonel turned to Greg. "Call all mobile units back to the base to pick up the package." He turned to Zack. "How much do we have?"

"A lot." Zack smiled.

As the mobile units dispersed to sprinkle the unzombifying agent around the city's perimeter, Rice chuckled to himself and looked at Zack.

"What's so funny?"

"Operation: Scatterbrains," Rice said with a smirk.

"You're so corny," Zack told his buddy, laughing as he said it.

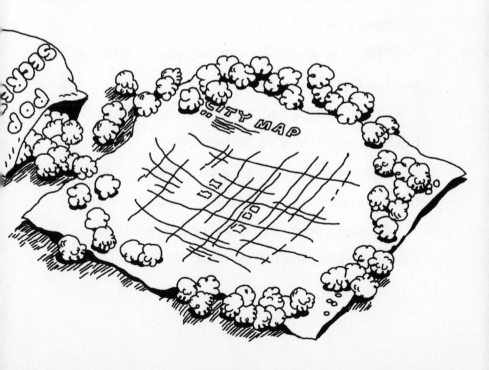

Just then, a large man wearing glasses and a doctor's smock jogged out of the front entrance of the hospital. "Colonel Briggs!" he yelled. "We've got problems, sir!"

"Yes, doctor," the colonel said.

"We've done everything we can, but our ginkgo supply is officially gone, and we've got zombies waking up from sedation."

"Dad?" Rice gasped and ran over to his father, giving him a great big bear hug.

"Johnston?" A lone tear trickled from Dr. Rice's eye. "I thought I'd never see you again . . ."

"Is Mom okay?" Rice asked.

"She's inside."

"Hey, Dr. Rice." Zack waved and handed his best buddy's dad a bag of popcorn.

"Zack!" Rice's dad greeted his son's BFF. "What's this?" he asked, looking at the popcorn.

"It's the antidote, Pop!" Rice explained. "Just feed it to the zombies, and they'll turn back into humans."

Dr. Rice opened up the bag and took a whiff. "Smells like brains," he said matter-of-factly.

"That was Madison's idea," Rice told him.

Dr. Rice nodded approvingly at Madison.

"Excuse me, Dr. Rice," Madison said. "You don't happen to know if my parents are alive, do you?"

"What are their names?" Dr. Rice asked.

"Frank and Julie Miller."

"Frank and Julie Miller," Rice's dad mumbled to himself. "We saw them last Friday night at the parent-teacher conferences. "

"So they're here?" Madison asked excitedly.

"No," he said. "I'm afraid the last time we saw them, your father was trying to bite into my wife's cranium," Dr. Rice told her apologetically. "Had to give him the old one-two." Rice's dad put up his dukes like an old-school boxer.

"Oh." Madison looked down, dejectedly.

"Don't worry, Madison," Zack said. "We'll go unzombify everyone at school after we get our mom and dad from the bank."

"Good idea, little bro," Zoe said. "Come on." She and Madison went outside and grabbed a few bags of the popcorn.

"You comin', Rice?" Zack asked.

"Not right now," Rice said. "I'm gonna go say whatsup to my mom."

"Cool," Zack said. "We'll be back in a little while."

"I know you will, dude," Rice said. He and Zack clasped hands, and Rice brought Zack in for a full-on man hug. "Thanks for, you know, saving my life, dude."

"Anytime, buddy!" Zack said, patting him on the back.

As Zack, Zoe, Madison, and Twinkles walked out of the hospital, UnNotGreg Bansal-Jones approached them. "I don't know who you guys are," the amnesiac ex-bully said, saluting them. "But if it weren't for you, we wouldn't have made it. So thanks." Then he marched off.

"Looks like you knocked some sense into him, Zack," said Madison, smiling.

"Guess so," Zack said, as they passed the command center. Ozzie leaned over a foldout table, studying a large map of the area, while the colonel directed Operation: Scatterbrains on the military radio.

"Later, Oz!" Zoe called to their friend.

Ozzie looked up. "Where are you guys going?"

"To get our parents," Madison said. "We'll be back."

"Cool," Ozzie said. He stood up tall and gave all four of them a formal salute.

"Get over here," Zack said, walking to Ozzie. He smiled and slapped him five.

Madison and Zoe came over, too. "See you in a bit, Oz," Madison said, giving Ozzie a friendly hug.

"Just don't *get* bit," said Ozzie, who now went to hug Zoe farewell, too.

But Zoe just stood there, holding out her fist.

"I'm not a hugger," she said. Ozzie laughed and bumped her fist.

"Later, buddy!" Zack waved good-bye for now as they strolled back to the Winnebago. Twinkles trotted at their heels.

"You guys ready?" asked Zack back in the RV.

Zoe revved the engine. "Look who you're askin' . . ."

The beat-up Winnebago rattled noisily. "Ready, Mad?"

"Ready, Freddy," Madison said.

"Arf!" Twinkles barked.

With that, they drove off down the dark Phoenix street.

And all was well.

Well . . . almost.

ACKNOWLEDGMENTS

Special thanks to Sara Shandler, Josh Bank, Rachel Abrams, Elise Howard, Katie Schwartz, and Lucy Keating, without whose sound zombie-chasing advice these books would not have been possible.

—J. K.